W9-BOA-812

Property of
Saint Mary School
Bethel, CT

Belle Pruitt

BY VERA AND BILL CLEAVER

Delpha Green & Company
Dust of the Earth
Ellen Grae
Grover
Hazel Rye
I Would Rather Be a Turnip
The Kissimmee Kid
Lady Ellen Grae
A Little Destiny
Me Too
The Mimosa Tree
The Mock Revolt
Queen of Hearts
Trial Valley
Where the Lilies Bloom
The Whys and Wherefores of Littabelle Lee

BY VERA CLEAVER

Moon Lake Angel
Sugar Blue
Sweetly Sings the Donkey

Belle Pruitt

VERA CLEAVER

HarperCollins*Publishers*

Belle Pruitt
Copyright © 1988 by Vera Cleaver
All rights reserved. No part of this book may be
used or reproduced in any manner whatsoever without
written permission except in the case of brief quotations
embodied in critical articles and reviews. Printed in
the United States of America. For information address
HarperCollins Children's Books, a division of
HarperCollins Publishers, 10 East 53rd Street,
New York, NY 10022.

Library of Congress Cataloging-in-Publication Data
Cleaver, Vera.
    Belle Pruitt.

    Summary: When her adored baby brother suddenly
dies of pneumonia, eleven-year-old Belle is left to
cope with the devastating effects on her family.
    [1. Death—Fiction.   2. Family problems—Fiction.
3. Family life—Fiction]   I. Title.
PZ7.C57926Be 1988   [Fic]   87-45879
ISBN 0-397-32304-2
ISBN 0-397-32305-0 (lib. bdg.)

Typography by Al Cetta
2 3 4 5 6 7 8 9 10

Belle Pruitt

Chapter One

AT THE AGE of eleven Belle Pruitt was a gold-star student as long as she wasn't asked to do anything creative. When that happened, she would start thinking about a history or science fact, about the signers of the Declaration of Independence or how many miles there were in a light-year. She read the newspaper once or twice a week and thought that when she got grown she might become a reporter of facts. To create was not a part of her nature, so after a page of words or a few quick strokes she would sit gazing out a window or at the back of somebody's head until

[3]

she was told to lay down her pencil or her brush.

The characters in the stories she wrote in her writing class were stick people. They smiled a lot. Occasionally one of them would come to life long enough to utter something such as "Oh" or "That is amazing." They were not amazed because they hadn't been given anything to be amazed about. They were failures and she was told so. The boxes she drew were a different matter. They were the only things she knew how to draw. They didn't slump or lean.

"They're my kind of art," Belle told her father. "The thing I like about them is you don't have to guess what they are, like you do when you look at something that's supposed to be a cloud only it's something else. Isabel Clark said her cloud was a little lost child looking for God, and everybody but me believed her. I thought it was a cloud. That's what I see when I look at one. When you look at a cloud, what do you see?"

[4]

"A cloud," replied her father. "When I look at a cloud, that's what I see." He was a rural mail carrier, and when out on his route would sometimes swap weather forecasts with his patrons. Clouds were a part of the forecasts. That was the only reason he stopped his work long enough to look at them. He was forty-two years old and saw things as Belle saw them—with a practical eye.

Belle's father had two living relatives—Aunt George and her twelve-year-old son, Ronald. When Ronald was eight his father decided that being a father and a husband weren't all he had been promised they would be and that life in the coal mines of West Virginia would be easier. So every month now Aunt George received a money order from him. Once in a while she wept a mild tear for what might have been, but secretly she enjoyed being a divorced woman. She thought that it gave her a dash of class. Her name was Georgia, but to the Pruitts she was Aunt George.

In Ronald, Aunt George had a problem yet

to be solved. When she came for a visit with the Pruitts, she usually left him at home to practice his flute lessons. When he did come with her, he wandered throughout the house, peering and poking into closets and drawers. He had an unearthly laugh and the habit of sidling up to Belle to whisper vulgar suggestions. They were not to be discouraged with words, so one Sunday afternoon when she had had enough of them, she hauled off and with a heavy book hit him over the head with such savage strength that he was seized with the blind staggers and had to lie on the couch for ten minutes.

The others came to crowd around. They wanted to know what had happened.

Belle looked at her parents and looked away. She was positive they didn't know about the things Ronald suggested and she didn't want them to learn of them from her, so she said, "I hit him."

"Why?" asked her father.

"Because I felt like it," answered Belle.

Ronald sat up. The color had come back into his face and his eyes had straightened themselves out. Slyly he said, "It wasn't anything. We were just horsing around. I brought my flute. Do you all want to hear my latest piece?"

After the flute piece and after Aunt George and Ronald went home, Belle's mother wanted to know why Belle couldn't get along with Ronald.

"He treats me like I'm dumb dust," growled Belle.

Her mother and father thought that was funny. Darwin, her little brother, beat on the tray of his high chair with his spoon.

These people were Belle's rewards. Blithe and vibrant, still youthful at forty, her mother was a care giver, the one who kept the home wheels oiled. No problem was too small or too big for her attention. A fixer of problems, she gave herself to her busy, sometimes rambunctious life without stint and with wit and grace. Her ready wit was her most attractive feature.

The day Darwin took his first two steps, it scared him so badly he screamed, and Mr. Pruitt and Belle laughed. "Don't laugh," said Mrs. Pruitt, controlling her own laughter. "After this the child may never learn to walk."

He did, of course, and now twenty months old he was the gold-wrapped chocolate, the one in the center of the birthday box. In loud competition with Mr. Pruitt he learned how to bray "Here Come the Animals Two by Two," and Mrs. Pruitt said he was surely headed for a career on the operatic stage. Darwin and Mr. Pruitt were buddies, even as Belle and her father were buddies.

Home was a little sloppy, the way everybody liked it, and was tender and comfortable. It meant tenderness and comfort. It wasn't young, so some of its floors squeaked and in a hard wind its panes rattled, but it was always there, faithful, unchanging, a part of the living world.

The Pruitts' five-bedroom home stood alone at the end of a dirt road on a spread of ground that was, except for its immediate lawn, the do-nothing kind. During the growing season the lawn was mowed and raked but after that it was ignored. The ground that lay beyond it was ignored. It was valuable in only one respect: Since the Pruitts owned it, no one else could build on it.

Belle didn't know what she had done to deserve these rewards except that she didn't back-talk her parents, told only little no-account lies, didn't use bad words and didn't whine after things that were out of reach of the family pocketbook. In all but her school studies she was a shirker of work, but if the tactics were right, she could be pressed into it.

She had learned there were two kinds of people in the world: those who have and those who have not. In moments of suffering over some trivial disappointment or hardship she admitted with a twinge of shame that she envied the "haves." They had everything and were so attractive and sure of themselves.

The "have nots" weren't always so attractive, the way they crept around with such hangdog expressions, hoping somebody would notice their misery and offer them a way out of it. They didn't have to look that way. The little purse Belle carried to school contained only her comb and lunch money, but she didn't hangdog it.

Neither did her brother Taylor, who was another "have not." He worked for a dairy, and as two of his employee benefits he was furnished with a worker's cottage to live in and the use of a pickup. When he and his wife Arlene came to town they came in the pickup. Arlene had a pair of pink elbow-length gloves she wore to the movies on Saturday nights. They were a present from Belle's sister Nettie. Once a year Nettie went through her closets and gave Arlene all of her cast-offs.

Nettie was one of the "haves." She was twenty years old and married to Hamp Greer, and she lived in the better part of Cold Springs. From the Greer house on clear days anybody with good eyesight could look out and see, in the blue distance, where Florida left off and Alabama began, just over the bluff there. Hamp was part owner of a furniture factory and was eighteen years older than Nettie.

Taylor and Arlene did not have any children, nor did Nettie and Hamp.

"We can't afford children," said Arlene, holding Darwin on her lap to tell him again about the cows at the dairy. Having seen them, he was always eager for news of them. Eyes glowing, he would lick Arlene's arm or her chin and say, "More. More." After the cow news he would let Arlene brush his hair.

Nettie said she and Hamp didn't want children. "Little rug apes," she said. "They're always pulling on something or chewing on something. You can't shut them up and they're never still. I can't stand them." She said that, yet when she came, she made a big fuss over Darwin. She never came without bringing a toy for him to float in his bath water. She would sit on the edge of the tub watching him slap the water. *"Coo ah,"* he would say, making the little rubber boat dance. When he tired of that, Nettie would take him up, dry him and dress him. Lovingly, he would rest his head against her shoulder, and she would say, "I need a hug. Who is going to give me one?"

Darwin would raise up to give his sober answer. "Darwin will." He didn't do any fooling around when it came to displays of affection. At family get-togethers he would totter from chair to chair passing out his hugs and kisses as if they were cookies on a plate.

It was Mrs. Pruitt who insisted on the family's social gatherings and made them festive.

Her Christmas and Thanksgiving feasts were served and eaten with a touch of ceremony.

That year on the morning of Easter Sunday the Pruitts prepared to cook chicken pilau. Taylor and Arlene came early and brought the chickens ready for boiling. Mr. Pruitt and Taylor built a fire in a cleared spot over on the weedlot while Mrs. Pruitt and Arlene cooked pots of rice on the kitchen stove.

Taylor brought the three-legged iron cauldron from the house to be hung over the outdoor fire. Into it, when all was ready to be mixed, would go the richly seasoned rice and the cooked chicken.

Nettie came alone and gave Darwin his Easter present, a yellow rubber duck. Clutching it, he teetered off to the bathroom, looked into the dry tub and said, "Broke."

Belle ran several inches of water into the tub and set the duck and Darwin in it. He loved being naked, loved to make the water splash and wave, loved the way the duck bobbed away from him. When it came back to him, he grabbed it and kissed it. "*Coo ah*," he said, chuckling his gleeful triumph.

From the open doorway Mrs. Pruitt called for Nettie to come with the camera. The picture taken of Darwin that day was the last one taken of him.

In May the Pruitts' part of Florida had a blackberry winter, a spell of cold weather in late spring when the blackberries are in bloom. The air tingled with the chill, and Mr. Pruitt reported that several people on his mail route were down with bad colds and flu. In his breakfast chair Darwin coughed. Two days later he was taken to the Cold Springs hospital, where he died of pneumonia.

The day that happened, Belle's father and mother were waiting for her when she came from school. Her father took her hands in his and told her. In the first horror of this there was disbelief, then rage. She flung her father's hands from her and kicked him and then tried to sink her teeth into the back of his hand.

His hands held her fast. She kicked him again, pulled away from him and turned to her mother.

Her mother's face was a blind, pale mask. "I will never," she said, "believe in anything good again."

The house then was so quiet, quiet as time. Big and capable, Aunt George came without Ronald, and bustled to the kitchen to make thick stews and corn bread. She didn't invite the Pruitts to eat what she cooked—she commanded them.

Nettie was there, as were Taylor and Arlene. They looked at one another and looked away. Belle devoured what was placed in front of her, slipped from her chair and went to the bathroom to cry into a towel. She wore her best dress to the funeral but forgot its belt. Mrs. Pruitt said the belt didn't matter.

When the little casket with the flowers on its top was lowered into its grave, Nettie moaned, and Arlene would have run forward but Taylor pulled her back. Impassively, Mrs.

Pruitt stood with one gloved hand on Mr. Pruitt's arm and the other raised to shade her bitter eyes from the sunlight.

Belle thought she had never seen anything so hideous as the cemetery or heard anything so hideous as the minister's prayer. After the funeral he came to sit in the Pruitts' living room with Mr. and Mrs. Pruitt for a while.

Others came, the way people do in a time of grief. In hushed tones they talked about how they knew what it was to suffer as the Pruitts were suffering because they too had lost dear ones.

Belle's father thanked them. Her mother did not. Listening, she sat with her hands folded, and the faraway look in her dry eyes deepened.

Those others who came brought so many pies and casseroles that Arlene had to ask them to stop. She and Nettie put all of Darwin's toys and clothes in boxes, and Taylor and Arlene took them away. Nettie went home then. So did Aunt George. Mr. Pruitt went back to work, and Belle went back to school.

The weather had warmed, but still Belle's mother wore a heavy sweater around the house. She would not sleep in a bed but spent her nights on the sofa in the living room. At night, when the rest of the house was dark, the floorboards in the living room creaked under her light back-and-forth tread. Meals were sketchy: cheese, ready-to-eat meats, canned fruits and grocery bread.

One day Belle came home to find her mother in the little room that had been Darwin's. Standing on a stepladder and using only the blade of a table knife, she was prying the bright nursery wallpaper from the walls piece by stubborn piece and dropping the pieces into a bag. She was working at this as though it was something she had to do, something that she was being made to do. Not a sliver of the paper must be left on the wall. It all had to come off. On her ladder, Mrs. Pruitt looked down at Belle. "Don't you see?"

Striving to understand, to see, Belle looked

[17]

back and saw her mother's flushed face as that of a stranger's. And, comprehending in the eerie way people her age sometimes do comprehend things beyond their years, she was afraid. Mama, she thought, has gone away from us. "Yes, I see," she said.

That evening, before dark, when she sat on the porch with her father, she told him, "Mama is different."

"She's coping with what has happened," said Mr. Pruitt. "We all are."

"I think we ought to find someplace else for us to live," said Belle. "This house won't let Mama forget that Darwin was here."

Her father looked out across the lawn to the weedlot. An hour before, it had rained just hard enough and long enough to dampen what struggled there: clumps of dog fennel, stands of old briar and patches of fermenting weeds. The wind blew across it now, bringing with it a sour odor.

"Your mother and I bought this place the

year after we were married," said Mr. Pruitt. "She wouldn't give it up."

"Then something else has got to happen," said Belle. "I thought of something if you want to hear it."

"I want to hear it," said Mr. Pruitt.

"It's about Aunt George," said Belle. "If you asked her to come and stay with us for a while, I think she would. She'd be good for Mama. She'd cook. And make Mama eat. And make her sleep in her bed."

Inside the house, in the room that had been Darwin's, a light had come on.

"She's at it again," said Belle.

Mr. Pruitt rose, walked to the edge of the porch and stood leaning against one of its posts. "If Aunt George came to stay with us until things are better around here, Ronald would have to come too."

Belle's shudder came, and went. "Yes, he would have to. Aunt George wouldn't leave him at home by himself."

[19]

The next day was a Saturday, a school holiday for Belle but a workday for Mr. Pruitt. Ordinarily Belle and her mother did the heavy weekly housecleaning on Saturdays, but this morning, after breakfast, Mrs. Pruitt carried what was left of her coffee to Darwin's room and closed the door.

Mr. Pruitt exchanged bleak looks with Belle. "You're right. We need some help," he said, and went after Aunt George and Ronald.

They came prepared to stay awhile. "For as long as we're needed," bellowed Aunt George.

She took charge. She went into Darwin's room and, while Belle and Ronald looked on, brought Mrs. Pruitt out. They stood in the hall with their arms around each other. As if it were something valuable, Mrs. Pruitt still held the table knife.

"Honey," said Aunt George, "I've come to take care of you."

"I don't need you to take care of me," said Mrs. Pruitt.

"Give me the knife," coaxed Aunt George.

[20]

"You're going to go to your room and go to bed."

Mrs. Pruitt drew back. "No. I haven't finished taking the paper off the walls in Darwin's room. It's got to come off. All of it."

Aunt George took the knife from Mrs. Pruitt and handed it to Belle. "Ronald and Belle will finish it."

Under his breath Ronald grunted, but he went to Darwin's room with Belle and sat on the window ledge watching her work at removing the wallpaper. He hummed and came to stand next to her to talk about girls. And the way he talked about them, the way he sucked on his dirty knowledge of them, made Belle shrink into herself.

Ronald saw her disgust and laughed his grating laugh. He went after his flute, wandered out into the front yard and sat under the loquat tree, serenading the empty air until Aunt George called him in and called Belle to the living room. One of its windows was stuck and she wanted it unstuck. She wanted the whole house open so that the fresh air and sunshine could come in. "All of this gloom in here," she said. "Put up the shades, Belle."

"Nettie told me to leave them down," said Belle. "She said the sun fades the rug. Her house has got drapes that cover all the windows and she never opens them except at night or when it rains."

"Nettie's house makes me think of a jail I saw one time," said Aunt George. "Ronald was just a little tyke then. We were traveling through Georgia and Ronald's father, he was driving, got pulled off to the side of the highway for speeding. The policeman's name was Proffitt and he said did we want to pay the forty dollars then or send it in. We said we didn't want to do either one, so off we went to the jail. They locked Ronald's father up but they let me sit in their waiting room until one of us could think of where we were going to get forty dollars."

"They brought in another criminal while we were there," crowed Ronald. "He had on alligator-skin shoes. They didn't lock him up. My old man was wearing tennis shoes."

"Why," exclaimed Aunt George, "how can you remember that? You weren't but five years old."

"I remember it," said Ronald.

"I remember how that place smelled," said Aunt George. "Like disinfectant. It was as clean as Nettie keeps her house but it looked a little homier. The one time Nettie asked me to her house, I was afraid to sit down for fear I might break something. I did break a glass. It slipped right out of my hand. I thought Nettie would have a green hemorrhage."

"She pays thirty-two dollars apiece for her glasses," said Belle. "They're crystal."

"Her being married to that old man she's married to and having to jump every time he belches, Nettie pays more than that for her glasses," said Aunt George. "But she'd rather be hanged from a rafter than admit it. Anyway, it's too late. That young man she jilted in favor of Hamp Greer has gone off to one of those countries south of here to teach the people how to be like us. I forgot the name of what he joined so he could do that."

"It was the Peace Corps, Ma," prompted Ronald, and rolled his eyes.

"Yes," said Aunt George. "That was the name of it. I wonder how that boy made out with it. I forgot his name. I remember how sweet his smile was."

"His name was Corky Wolfe and he didn't have any money," said Belle. "If Nettie had married him instead of Hamp, she'd be drinking her iced tea out of jelly glasses now."

"There are worse things," declared Aunt George. And said, "Put the shades up in here and let the sun come in." She didn't ask what rooms she and Ronald would occupy. She went to the back of the house and for herself chose Nettie's old room.

Ronald moved into the room where Taylor had spent many a midnight and post-midnight hour hunched over his correspondence course studies. He was convinced he could become someone better than an apprentice plumber, that he could become one of those well-dressed men who carries a briefcase to work instead of a lunch box. He believed he could overcome the stigma of being a high school dropout and become an accountant. His heart ran fast when he thought of this future. It ran faster the evening he went with a friend to a square dance and met Arlene.

Taylor didn't know how to dance. He had only come to watch those who did. But Arlene, quick on her feet and graceful as a reed, drew him out onto the dance floor where he had performed brilliantly.

After that Taylor had become impatient with his books and papers. He lived only for the ring of the telephone. Night after night Arlene teased him away from his studies, so temporarily he put them away. He told himself that his career as an accountant could wait, and steamed out to Holland's Dairy where he landed a grown man's job with a grown man's pay. A week later he married Arlene. Her mother and father had a chimpanzee act with a traveling circus, and couldn't come for the wedding. They sent a box containing pictures of Arlene when she had been a part of their act.

Taylor still owed Hamp Greer a hundred and twenty-five dollars of the three hundred he had borrowed to buy Arlene's engagement and wedding rings. Sometimes at night when he was too tired to sleep or when it was too hot for sleep he would get up, go out to his porch, sit there with his bare feet on its railing and think about the little scarred desk in the corner of his room at home. Now when he worked at his studies, his desk was the kitchen table.

Taylor's desk had become Ronald's, but Ronald didn't use it as Taylor had. It was his meal table.

Mealtimes in the Pruitt home had always been a time for sharing the adventures or misadventures of the day. But now the intimacy of this was gone because Aunt George and

Ronald were there, and because Mrs. Pruitt contributed little to the table talk. She came from her room wearing an old shapeless robe and without bothering to comb her hair or wash the sleep from her eyes. Looking like a little rumpled owl, she sat, with her head lowered, where Aunt George told her to sit. Every now and then she would raise her head and half turn in her chair, as if listening to a sound from another room. When that happened, Belle's father would quickly ask somebody an awkward question or would speak of something impersonal.

Ronald didn't want to sit with the others or speak of anything. That Saturday evening after all were seated, he prowled around the table, plate in hand, reaching over the shoulders of the others to spear the biggest piece of fried chicken, the fattest biscuit, the longest ear of corn. When he ladled peas over all of this, Mrs. Pruitt looked up at him but didn't speak.

Ronald took his plate to his room.

"Maybe the boy is feeling a little out of place," suggested Mr. Pruitt.

"He's a sensitive child," said Aunt George. "He's emotional. He feels things most people don't. I guess it all ties in with his talent, which is not always easy to live with, but I'd rather he'd be the way he is than coarse like some boys his age are."

Mr. Pruitt buttered an ear of corn for Mrs. Pruitt and laid it on her plate. She wasn't eating. He pretended not to notice, and looked across the table at Belle. "What were you telling us, Belle?"

Belle took up her interrupted tale. "I was telling you that this coming Monday is the last day of school, so everybody is going to go to the Strand Theater and see a special movie. It's educational. My class is going to sit in the front row because we've got the highest average grades."

"How nice," murmured Mrs. Pruitt. She still wasn't eating.

"Before it starts," said Belle, "Ronald is

going to get up on the stage and play a piece on his flute."

"He told me," said Aunt George. "And I'd be proud to go and hear him if I was invited. But Ronald never wants me to hear him play in public. He says if he knew I was listening he'd be nervous."

"Anybody can come who wants to," said Belle. "It's free."

"I'll be working, and I wouldn't want your mother to go by herself," said Mr. Pruitt.

"Ronald is shy," said Aunt George.

About as shy as a thunderbolt but not as smart, thought Belle. Thunderbolts know when to quit. Ronald doesn't.

The door to her room didn't have a lock, so before she climbed into her bed that night, she pushed a cedar chest against it and then tied three empty tin cans to a length of heavy twine and hung them on the inside knob. After that she felt a little safer, and lay with her hand under her cheek, waiting for sleep to come.

There were night sounds, those of an insect buzzing against the window screen and then that of her father going through the house, safety-checking it for the night.

Belle got up, turned on her light, went to the door and cautiously, so that the cans wouldn't make a noise, opened it a crack. At the end of the hallway her father, ready for his bed, turned and said, "Good night again, Belle, and this time I mean it. Go back to your bed and go to sleep. Stop your worrying. Your mother is all right. Everything is all right."

Vastly she wanted to believe him, and because he sounded so sure, believing was possible then.

The darkness in her room was not precisely black, and she lay facing the door, watching it and listening for the jiggle of the cans. She thought that if she heard them jiggle just once or saw the door move even a fraction of an inch, she would leap from her bed and snatch Ronald bald-headed. He was bigger and stronger than she, but he wouldn't be expecting her to come at him like that.

Belle lay in the dark organizing her inner self, weighing her ifs against her buts. After a while of this a drop of poison crept into her mind. She shoved it away, and it came back. She turned and faced the window. Beyond its glistening pane the world rolled in wet darkness. It was raining.

The force of the rain brought down a cluster of bronze-skinned fruit from the loquat tree in the front yard. Belle stepped over it the next morning when she went out to get her father his Sunday paper. The sky was pale, washed clean, bare from rim to rim except for one white high cloud. Belle looked at it once, and didn't look again. The cloud was a cloud: vapor. There was nothing mysterious about it. There was nobody in it looking for anything. It wouldn't do to think that there was, to start thinking about Darwin again, because once that got started there would be no end to it.

Belle stooped for the paper. Her father spent the morning with it. Her mother slept. Belle finished removing the paper from the walls in Darwin's room. In his room Ronald played his flute. Twice Aunt George had to tell him to stop, that there was somebody in the house who was resting.

Aunt George made lemon pie for Sunday dinner dessert but didn't use all the lemons in the refrigerator bin. On Monday morning when Belle left the house, she took all that were left with her. Before she wrapped them in waxed paper and tucked them into her handbag, she cut them into halves.

Her father didn't go to work at his usual time. He drove Belle and Ronald to the Strand Theater. Holding his flute, Ronald sat in the car's backseat. He wore the white suit and the red bow tie that he always wore when he was scheduled to get up on a stage and play to an audience. He was excited, and when Mr. Pruitt stopped the car in front of the theater, he was the first one out.

[32]

The Strand Theater catered only to evening theater-goers except when its civic-minded owner donated its use to daytime community functions. It was an old building, but its entrance was still an attractive invitation, and its acoustics were superior to those of the other public buildings in Cold Springs. Recently it had been renovated. Some of its plush seats had been replaced, and beneath its red carpeting there were sections of new flooring. Its front-most seats, those closest to the stage, were hard and new. Now, in one of them, Belle sat and waited for the theater to fill. Her classmates, most of them girls, occupied the front row. Isabel Clark sat next to her.

It was one of Isabel's habits to ask questions to which she already knew the answers. "When are they going to make it dark in here?"

"When it's time for the movie," said Belle. "First we're going to hear Ronald play."

"I hate his socks," said Isabel. "Only his mother could love him. Does she?"

"She thinks he's sensitive."

"I forgot his last name."

"It's Hunt."

"I thought it was McNasty," said Isabel. "I'd like to buy him for what he's worth and sell him for what he thinks he's worth. I'd be rich. How can you stand having him for your kin?"

"I didn't do it," said Belle.

"Does his mother know how he talks to girls?"

"I don't think so."

"Why don't you tell her?"

"Because she's his mother," said Belle.

Isabel looked like one of those birds that sits on an overhead wire waiting for something interesting to show up. "I didn't have time to eat breakfast. I wish I had something to eat."

"You want a piece of lemon?" asked Belle.

"Where would I get a piece of lemon?" said Isabel.

Belle opened the handbag on her lap, and Isabel leaned to gaze at what was in it. "Lemons. All cut up. They make my mouth squirt."

"Yes," said Belle.

Isabel looked up at the stage, then turned her head to lock eyes with Belle. There was a spirit-to-spirit exchange of looks. Said Isabel, "How many pieces in there?"

"Eight," said Belle.

"You should have brought more," hissed Isabel. "There won't be enough for everybody. But quick! Before one of the teachers comes."

The theater had filled. The student ushers were taking their seats, and the teachers theirs. The overhead lights on the stage came on. Followed by Ronald, his teacher came hurrying down the aisle, mounted the stage steps and stood looking down into the audience.

Her name was Elva Burke. She was the youngest and the prettiest member of the school's faculty. She had a passion for teaching but had days when she wished that she had chosen another profession. Ronald Hunt made her think that she might have been happier being one of those people who sit all day in a tree tower in a forest watching for fires.

Miss Elva Burke smiled. "Students, you all know Ronald Hunt and his beautiful music. This morning he is going to play for us. Shall we let him know how much we appreciate him?"

Politely the members of the audience clapped.

Elva Burke said, "Ronald, it's all yours." And left the stage and went back up the aisle.

Ronald stood bathed in light. The silver flute in his hands gleamed. Dramatically he moved as close to the edge of the stage as safety would allow, fastened his eyes on his frontline audience, raised his flute and began to play.

Belle raised her lemon half to her mouth, bit into it and sucked, drawing its juice into her mouth and rolling it around.

Ronald's eyes found her. He tried to set his look on what his fingers were doing, but it kept coming back to Belle. He began to have a hard time with his mouth. It looked as though he were trying to swallow it. It kept twisting, pulling first to one side and then to the other.

The students in the front row sucked their lemon pieces.

Ronald looked out over their heads, and for a fraction of a second his music was brave and sweet, but then on a high ripple of notes it stopped.

Ronald looked down into a row of delighted, hostile faces. He lowered his flute, drew his arm across his face, tried to laugh and failed. His enraged scream came. "You all stop that! You're messing me up!"

From her seat in the second section of the theater's tiered seats, Miss Elva Burke rose and almost ran back down the aisle to the stage. On the way she had a quick daydream. In it she saw herself sitting happily at a loom in a textile factory and when work was done happily going home to share her supper with a cat.

That evening supper at the Pruitt's house

was late because Nettie had been called to come and help solve a family crisis. On the porch she and Mr. Pruitt talked while Belle sat on the step with her hands in her lap. As though she had lost her power of being, Mr. Pruitt and Nettie talked around her.

"She's under house arrest," said Mr. Pruitt. "The principal at her school recommended it."

"But what did she do that's so bad?" asked Nettie. "On the phone you talked so fast I only understood about every third word."

"I sucked a lemon while Ronald was playing his flute for my school this morning," reported Belle. "I gave lemons to some of the other girls too. I handed them out and we all sucked them. We messed Ronald up. He had it coming to him."

"Why did he have it coming to him?" demanded Nettie.

"She won't say," said Mr. Pruitt.

Nettie walked to the steps, looked at the

top of Belle's head and went back to confront Mr. Pruitt. "Well, I don't know what you expect me to do. I don't know why you called me to come all the way over here."

"Your mother isn't well, and I can't have trouble between Belle and Ronald when I'm not here to stop it," said Mr. Pruitt. "It's bad enough when I'm here. You remember that time she hit Ronald and almost made him pass out?"

The day was nudging along toward evening. On the western horizon the sun was a fireball. Silently Belle spoke to its ancient light. *I did make him pass out. He was out for about ten minutes.* Aloud she said, "What to do is, you give me another chance. I won't hit Ronald again. I won't suck any more lemons while he's playing his flute. I'll behave. For Mama, I know I've got to. I don't know why I did what I did this morning. I didn't think I'd cause all of this trouble."

Mr. Pruitt and Nettie didn't hear. Nettie

made the bracelets on her arm clink. "If you're asking me what I'd do, I'll tell you. First I'd put Belle under house arrest."

"I am under house arrest," said Belle.

"And next take Mama to a psychiatrist," said Nettie. "He'll straighten her out."

"Your mother doesn't need a psychiatrist," flared Mr. Pruitt. "What she needs is a chance to get herself together again."

"And next send Aunt George and that kid of hers home," said Nettie. "I knew when you asked her to come that there would be trouble, and now you've got it. Get rid of it. Aunt George isn't needed here. Send her home."

"I am not going to send Aunt George home," declared Mr. Pruitt. "She's good for your mother. This afternoon, for the first time since Darwin died, she got your mother out of the house. They went for a walk."

Again Nettie made her bracelets rattle. Mr. Pruitt took her by her arm. "Come with me."

"Where?" asked Nettie.

"You and I are going to take a little walk," answered Mr. Pruitt.

They were gone for about ten minutes. They went only as far as the loquat tree, and stood there talking. When they came back, Mr. Pruitt immediately went into the house.

Nettie sat down on the step beside Belle. "Go to your room and get some of your things together. I'll wait here for you."

"Where are you going to take me?" said Belle.

"Home with me," said Nettie.

"I'm under house arrest," said Belle. "I can't go anywhere."

"You're going to come live with Hamp and me for a while," said Nettie.

Chapter Two

IT GREW DARK during the drive across town. The first distant star appeared and the streetlights came on. Nettie turned on the car's headlights and went around one corner so fast that she ran up onto a curb and had to back off. There was quite a bump to this, and Nettie said, "This is all so unnecessary. I don't know what Hamp is going to say about it."

"It was just a curb," said Belle. "You didn't hurt anything."

"Why is it you never get what I'm talking about?" said Nettie. "I meant I don't know what Hamp is going to say about you staying with us. I should have called him and asked him, but Dad had me so rattled that I didn't think about it. He's enough to rattle anybody. He's always so right. He thinks he is. There's no reasoning with him."

Like a lion that smells blood, Belle said, "You could still call Hamp. We could stop at a drugstore and you could phone him from there. Then if he says for me not to come, you could take me out to stay with Taylor and Arlene."

"Oh, sure," said Nettie. "So they could say that Hamp and I never want to help with anything. We'd never hear the end of it. Taylor borrows money from Hamp, and Arlene wouldn't have a decent rag to her back if it wasn't for me, but they still talk about us something terrible. You think I don't know that? I know that. They think we're a couple of saps."

"I don't think Arlene and Taylor would say you and Hamp never want to help," said

Belle. She was certain that was exactly what they would say. "And if they think you and Hamp are a couple of saps, they must be a couple themselves," she said. She didn't see how anybody could be a sap. Sap was the fluid part of a plant.

Nettie had stopped the car for a traffic light. She switched on the car's radio but almost at once switched it back off. "I just hope you can remember that living with Hamp and me is not going to be like living at home."

"I know it won't be," said Belle. She knew it all right. To go and spend an hour or two or a night at Nettie's house was one thing. It was going to be another to live there. She wasn't good enough to live there, not careful enough or quick enough. At Nettie's house the minute the last bite of a meal was swallowed, the dishes were snatched off the table. The instant a bath was finished, the tub had to be scoured. When Nettie made her beds, she pulled the bottom sheets so tight they were like boards. Not a wrinkle must show.

The corners had to be creased and then tucked in just so. Sleeping on one of Nettie's beds was like sleeping on the floor. Nettie's whole house was like her beds. To be sent to live in it was like being sent off to a prison.

"I can remember that living with you and Hamp is not going to be the same as living at home," said Belle.

"Hamp and I have our routines," said Nettie.

"All of us need routines," said Belle.

"We don't watch much television," said Nettie.

"Television makes idiots out of people," said Belle. She didn't think that it did. She watched television and she wasn't an idiot. Her mother and father watched it and they weren't idiots.

The traffic light had changed from red to green. During the remainder of the ride Belle sat as close to the door on her side as she could get. She actually hoped that its catch would suddenly weaken, causing it to fly open.

If that happened, she would be thrown out on the pavement, and if she hit just right, she might be lucky enough to crack her skull and get amnesia. Victims of it didn't die. They just smiled and were happy. Everything that had made them sad or mad was all wiped out. Lots of criminals got amnesia after their crimes caught up with them. The newspapers said so.

The door on the passenger's side of the car remained fastened. At an intersection an ambulance pulled up behind the car and then shot around it, lights flashing and siren screaming. Belle wished that she could be either the one in it or the one it was going after. Her brother-in-law was not going to howl with joy when he found out that she had come to live in his house. He would be polite at first, but as soon as that wore off he'd turn all sulky and gripey the way he did when Nettie dragged him to one of the family get-togethers and they stayed too long.

Hamp was in one of the big chairs in his

living room. He was wearing the baggy clothes he favored when at home. His shoes were off, and he was reading a newspaper. When Belle and Nettie entered the room, he lowered the paper and peered at them over the rims of his glasses.

"Surprise," said Nettie in a wan and humble voice. "I'm home and look who I've got with me."

Hamp stood and, in the same courteous way he always said it, said, "Hello, Belle. How are you?"

Belle wanted to lean against something. Instead she held herself at strict attention. "I'm in trouble at home for sucking a lemon while Ronald was playing his flute for my school this morning. Now everybody's mad at me. Aunt George told Dad she couldn't stay and help with Mama anymore unless he did something about me. That's why I'm here. But if you don't want me to stay, I can go out and live with Taylor and Arlene."

"What's this?" said Hamp.

More in disgust than in a spirit of helpfulness, Nettie said, "Oh, let me tell it. At home everything is in a mess. That's where I've been. That's why I'm late."

"I've been home since six o'clock," said Hamp.

"Well, I'm sorry," protested Nettie. "But none of this is my fault. Dad called me and I had to go over and see if I could help."

"Your family," said Hamp, who didn't have a family. "It's always something with them. I told you to tell your father to take your mother to a psychiatrist."

"I did tell him that," argued Nettie. "But he wouldn't listen. He said she doesn't need a psychiatrist. He refuses to take her to one. He's got that old-fashioned idea that the only people who go to psychiatrists are crazy."

"Mama is not crazy," said Belle, speaking to a floor lamp. "I don't think she needs a psychiatrist either."

"What do you think a psychiatrist is?" inquired Hamp.

"It's a doctor who gets paid to listen to somebody talk," said Belle. "That's what Arlene told me."

"A psychiatrist is a physician who treats mental disorders," said Hamp.

"Then Mama doesn't need one," said Belle, still addressing the lamp.

"Oh?" said Nettie. "Well, Miss Wisdom, what do you think she needs?"

"I don't know," admitted Belle. "It's something we haven't thought of yet. She's just trying to get over Darwin and it hurts. Don't you know how much it hurts?"

Nettie looked as if she had been hit in the face with a wet rag. She walked over to Hamp's shoes, picked them up and put them down. For a second she looked ready to cry, but then in a calm way, speaking to Hamp, she said, "Dad asked me if we could take Belle for a while and I had to say yes. Should I have said no?"

Hamp returned to his chair. He took off his glasses and, with the tail of his shirt, polished them. There was nothing gripping about his appearance. His hair stood up in front in a stiff tuft. In back of the tuft, where it left off and baldness began, there were strings of hair combed sideways over shiny pinkness. He was squat and paunchy. He was that kind of man who could sit behind a desk for a lifetime directing the lives of others and making decisions. He made a decision then. "You did," he said, "what you had to do. Belle will stay here with us. Take her upstairs and give her a room."

So began Belle's life with Hamp and Nettie. Her room was big and had its own bathroom. Her clothes went into one of the dresser's deep drawers. She had remembered to bring her toothbrush and toothpaste. She brushed her teeth, wiped the sink dry with toilet tissue and then sat huddled in the blue velvet chair beside the bed until Nettie called her to come down and make herself useful. It was late but Hamp still wanted a full-course dinner.

At the sink, Belle washed lettuce, peeled potatoes and oranges and put all the peelings, rinds and discarded leaves where Nettie told her to put them, in a rubber pail on the back porch. The pail had a lid and was almost full of other older damp kitchen refuse.

"What's it for?" asked Belle.

"For Pearl," answered Nettie, and rushed back to her dinner preparations.

It was almost ten o'clock before they ate. As they ate, Hamp and Nettie talked about a new gutter system for the house, whether it should be galvanized or aluminum. Hamp said that it should be aluminum because aluminum didn't rust. He said he had phoned the gutter man to that effect.

Belle thought that she shouldn't talk about anything, so she didn't. Instead she thought about Pearl. She decided that Pearl was a cute little pig that had wandered over from a farm in Alabama, and when Hamp and Nettie couldn't find out who it belonged to, they decided to keep it. To them, a pig was better

[51]

than a dog or a kid. It ate all their garbage
and never had to come into the house for
anything. Right now it was out there somewhere snoozing, keeping an eye on its mud
hole, waiting for the dark to go away and the
sun to come again. When that happened,
somebody would trot out with the pail of all
that good soured stuff that had been saved
for it.

Having settled the question of Pearl to her
mental satisfaction, Belle finished her dinner.
She had begun to feel a little better about
having to live with Hamp and Nettie. They
were kind. Their lives were different from
the one she was used to, but that was because
they thought differently.

Before she went up to bed, Belle thought
about kissing Hamp and Nettie good-night
but decided against it. It was a part of their
differentness that they weren't kissing people,
that they sat across from one another in the
silent living room. Hamp had his face buried
in his newspaper, and Nettie was copying

recipes from a magazine, transferring them onto little cards.

Nettie was a good cook. For breakfast the next morning she made French toast. "We always have it on Tuesday," she said, hurrying to fill Hamp's water glass and coffee cup. Dressed to go to his office, he came to the table and ate. He and Nettie talked some more about the gutter system. She brought a checkbook to the table, and Hamp wrote a check but said not to give it to the gutter man until the work was completed. Nettie said that the gutter man and his crew had promised to come at eight o'clock.

Nettie didn't want help with the dishes or with any of the other housework. "There's going to be a lot of commotion around here today," she said. "The best way you can help is to stay out of my way and the way of everybody else. Don't talk to the gutter men when they get here. Talking will slow them down, and Hamp wants the work they're going to do to be finished this morning. Can you find something to amuse yourself? Do you want to go see one of your friends?"

"I can't," said Belle. "I'm under house arrest."

"You can be under house arrest again when you get back," said Nettie, who wasn't particular about keeping rules as long as they weren't hers. "Just don't ask me to take you anywhere. I'm too busy."

"Pearl," said Belle, as if the thought of Pearl had just occurred to her. She had been thinking of little else since six o'clock. "I'll go see Pearl and take her her pail of garbage. She'll be glad to see me."

Nettie turned from the sink, where she was rinsing the breakfast dishes before putting them into the dishwasher. "I didn't know you knew Pearl."

"I know her," said Belle. "She's little and kind of pink. She's got short white hair and lives by a mud hole."

"You have the strangest ideas," said Nettie. "Pearl doesn't live by a mud hole. She lives in a house. It's down the road a mile from here. When you go up the hill you'll see it on the other side. It's the only one there, so you can't miss it. It's got a big garden in front. If you want to take what I've saved for her, go ahead but be sure and bring my pail back."

"Pearl's a human?" said Belle.

"Of course she's a human. What else would she be?"

"I thought she was a pig."

"She is not a pig. She's a human."

"If she isn't a pig," said Belle, "why am I going to take her pig garbage?"

"Pearl collects garbage," said Nettie, but didn't explain further. It was left to Pearl to do the explaining.

Belle found her in her garden, a jungle of plant life. The plants were everywhere, some of them growing in cans, some in the ground, some vegetable, some ornamental. There was

[55]

a ragged pathway, and along this were empty tin cans lying on their sides, and piles of what appeared to be old garbage.

At the end of the pathway there stood a woman. Both of her arms were bandaged from shoulder to wrist. Her right arm was in a loose kitchen towel sling tied at her shoulder blade so that the ends of it stood up like a rabbit's ears. She was gazing at a sprawled plant bed filled with stiff, green-and-white spokes. The spokes were tinged pink in their centers and had wicked-looking spikes sticking out from their edges.

As though every day a stranger came trudging into her garden lugging a rubber pail filled with kitchen garbage, the plant gazer turned from her study, looked around at Belle and said, "Bromeliads. And they bite. They multiply. I started out with one but now look. There must be half a dozen new ones. That old mother in there bit me. I was trying to separate some of her pups from her, and she bit me. Don't you go near it. It'll bite you too. I warn everybody who comes to stay away from it, but I didn't myself and now look what I've got. A bad skin infection in both arms. It's the spores that caused it, my doctor said."

Belle set the pail down in the pathway. "I'm Nettie Greer's sister, and if you're Pearl I've brought you some potato peelings and other stuff. I'm Belle Pruitt."

"I'm Pearl," said the plant lady, bestowing a pearly smile. Her interest in Belle was the kind given to a child who has brought a flower. The flower was lovely. It was wanted, but it shouldn't be grabbed from the child's hand. For bringing such a thoughtful gift the child herself deserved some attention. "You don't look much like Nettie," observed Pearl. "How come I've never seen you around here before?"

"Because I've never been around here much," said Belle. "Before, I only came for an hour or two, or to spend the night with Nettie. But now I'm going to live with her and Hamp for a while."

"Now isn't that just nifty," said Pearl.

"I'm supposed to take the pail back," said Belle.

Pearl bobbed her white head. "I know. Nettie always wants it back, but I can't empty it now. I can't do much of anything until my arms heal. Do you know, I haven't properly made my bed for a week? All I can do is yank it together. You see, I live alone."

Belle turned, looked at Pearl's house and turned back. "You live in this big place all by yourself?"

"Not by myself," said Pearl. "I live with my plants. They talk to me. Whenever I think that life hasn't been as good to me as it should have been and that it's no good anyway because all of it ends sooner or later, I come out here and my plants talk to me. They tell me how wrong I am."

"If I ever heard a plant talk, I'd run," said Belle. "I'd know I was crazy."

"There is no end to life," said Pearl. "That's what my plants tell me."

Oh, fruit, thought Belle. I came here to deliver a pail of pig garbage and now not only am I going to have to empty it but make this crazy old lady's bed too. She didn't want to do either. What she wanted to do was to take her empty pail, go back to the road and amble along it until she found a quiet place where she could sit for a while and brood.

Belle took in a breath. "I'll make your bed if you want me to and empty the pail too. Where do you want me to dump it? What's it for?"

Instantly Pearl was all grateful eagerness. "The pail first. What's in it is for my compost pile. Come. I'll show you."

The compost pile lay on a spread of open ground at the far end of the garden where there were no plants, only pest weeds and patches of dried cracked mud. The whole area had a stranded look.

Following Pearl out to the compost pile, Belle looked at this wasteland and thought of the Pruitts' do-nothing piece of land where once she had dug a "shirk ditch" four feet long and three feet deep. Digging it had been work, but when completed, it had been her refuge from work, her loafing place. Until its sides caved in and the weeds took it back, she had whiled away many an escaped hour in that ditch.

To Pearl's back Belle said, "We've got some property that looks like this part of your garden."

Pearl's skirt had caught a thorn. She checked her stride long enough to pick it off and then lifted her head to lovingly survey what was hers. "Isn't it beautiful?"

"Beautiful," said Belle. She didn't think it was beautiful. She thought it looked uncivilized and that what it needed was one of those big trucks with a shovel on its front to come in, scoop everything up, run it down to Key West and sling it into the ocean. The compost pile needed the same treatment.

Pearl gloated over her compost pile. "I build a new one every year. When this one is ready, my plants will eat it up."

"You're going to feed this garbage to your garden?" said Belle.

"It isn't garbage," rejoiced Pearl. "It's compost."

Belle removed the lid to her pail. "You want me to string this stuff around the sides of this pile or put in on top or what?"

"Put it on top," directed Pearl. "And then we'll add a little commercial fertilizer and some soil. Then you'll want to moisten the whole thing—but don't soak it. There's a bag of fertilizer around here someplace. Maybe I left it over there in the weeds. My little digger tool should be inside the bag. See if you can find it."

Belle left the pail and the compost pile and went sprinting off through the weeds looking for the bag of fertilizer. It had been opened, and a short-handled garden tool shaped like a scoop was inside it. The bag was heavy and had to be dragged back to the compost pile.

In a frenzy of activity, working at Pearl's direction, Belle added the refuse from the pail to the compost pile, added scoops of fertilizer, dug soil and added that.

Pearl forgot her sick arms, tried to hug herself, winced and laughed. "Now the water. Then you'll need to fork the whole thing so that the moisture can get to the dry parts. Do you see a rake or a garden fork around here? And the hose. I think it's back there in the garden."

Belle looked around but didn't see anything but some anthills, the bare ground around the compost pile and the weeds. Pearl sent her back to the garden for the fork and the hose. The hose was long and heavy and kinked. Every few feet it had to be unkinked.

Pearl said that she wished she could help.

"I don't need any help," Belle shrieked.

She licked sweat from her upper lip and tasted dirt. By this time the full hot sun was up.

The only way Pearl helped was to go back to where the hose was connected to a spigot and turn on the water. She wanted a concave place made on top of the compost pile. "To catch the rainwater. It will seep down into the dry parts."

The work on the compost pile took an hour. After that, there was still Pearl's bed to be made.

"But you must be tired," sympathized Pearl. "So let's let the bed go till tomorrow. You can come back tomorrow and make it for me."

"I'm not a bit tired," said Belle. "You want me to use these same sheets or put on clean ones?"

Pearl said that clean ones would be nice, showed Belle where to find them and went to her kitchen.

Belle attacked the bed. She removed the rumpled sheets and spread the clean ones, drawing the bottom sheet tight and then smoothing the top one over it. She was a member of The Sunshine Girls and had done what any of the other members would have done—aided an old sick person.

The smell of compost clung to her. She was strong, but her muscles were not accustomed to so much exertion. Now those in the backs of her legs quivered. On her way back to Nettie's she stooped to pinch them. And when their quivering didn't stop she gave them some hard punches with her fist.

The road in back of her and in front of her lay in dry summery emptiness. It was its emptiness she noticed most, and raised her head to stare into it. Promising nothing, it stared back.

Chapter Three

AT LUNCH Belle told Nettie she was cured
of wanting to fight with Ronald. It was one
o'clock, and the gutter men had finished their
work. They had pulled their truck around to
the back of the house and were loading the
old rusted gutters onto the truck's bed.

"So I'm ready to go back home now," said
Belle.

"Wait just a minute," said Nettie. "I can't
talk and read too. I want to finish this story."
She had her face buried in a romance magazine, holding it up in front of her face with

her left hand. With her right hand she groped for her corned beef sandwich.

Belle waited until she could wait no longer. Then with a little clank she laid her fork on her plate. "So do you want to take me or should I walk or what?"

Nettie lowered her magazine. She was especially fond of the love stories in the romance magazines where the husbands were young and good-looking. She wouldn't allow herself to cheat and see how the stories ended, so until she got to the last page, she didn't know that the one she was reading didn't end at all. She was irritated with it. "I'll have to wait until next month to see how it ends. I don't know why the people who publish this stuff do that."

"They do it," said Belle, "so you'll buy their magazine next month to find out. I can tell you how it ends. They're all the same. Isabel Clark buys new ones every month, and she let me read some of them. In the end the girl or the man does something to make the suffering stop. One of them has to do something or the suffering wouldn't stop. That's the way it is in real life too."

"How is it you know so much about suffering and real life?" asked Nettie.

"I want to go home," said Belle in a dogged voice.

"You can't," said Nettie. "I told Dad I'd keep you here until things with Mama got better." She left the table long enough to go to the kitchen door and hand the gutter-crew foreman his check. When she came back to the table, she spoke in a softer way. "You can't go home to stay, but I tell you what. My bridge club is going to meet here tomorrow. As soon as we've finished here, I'm going to drive over to Mama's and invite her to come too. If you want to go with me, you may. Just please don't have any trouble with Ronald while we're there."

"Mama doesn't know how to play bridge," said Belle.

"Remind me to look in her closet and see

if her good white dress is clean," said Nettie. "None of the girls in my club have met her, and I want her to make a good impression on them."

If Mama showed up at your bridge club wearing a tin can, she'd make a good impression on those bridge girls, thought Belle.

During the two o'clock ride across town with Nettie, she started practicing what she hoped was a meek look for Aunt George's benefit. Experience wasn't on her side. Her efforts produced a frozen grimace.

It was out of the way, but to reach the Pruitts' place Nettie drove through one of Cold Spring's tackiest neighborhoods. The houses there were the dreary look-alike structures such as factory workers the world over live in. In front of one of them Nettie slowed the car for a second. "That's where Corky Wolfe used to live. He worked for Hamp then. When I was eighteen I had a crush on Corky that wouldn't quit."

"What did he look like?" asked Belle.

"Like he was young and broke," answered Nettie. Then, as if fleeing from something, she stepped down hard on the gas.

Belle continued to practice her meek look. When she and Nettie got to the Pruitts' house, it took Aunt George a few minutes to notice it. Dressed to go out, she had on her brown dress and brown shoes but said she couldn't find her hat.

"Nobody wears hats anymore," said Nettie.

"I always wear mine when we go to the cemetery," said Aunt George. "It keeps the sun off my face. When we get there, the taxi driver can't drive in. He lets us out at the gate and we have to walk in. I don't like the sun in my face."

"The cemetery," said Nettie in a hollow voice.

"Your Mama is getting dressed to go now," said Aunt George. "I haven't called for the taxi yet. Now that you're here, you can save your mother that expense and drive us." She,

Belle and Nettie were in the Pruitts' living room. Its window shades weren't all the way up. Aunt George lumbered over to them, put them all the way up and returned to sit between Nettie and Belle on the sofa.

"I like lots of light in the house," she said. "It makes things cheerful."

"It also fades the rug," said Nettie. "Hamp and I gave Dad and Mama the rug in here. We paid a lot of money for it. It didn't come from any outlet store."

"I do most of my shopping at outlet stores," said Aunt George. "That's where I get all of my clothes and Ronald's."

"Where," Belle dared to ask, "is Ronald?"

"Gone swimming," replied Aunt George. "And if he gets back here while you're here, you're not to start any trouble. I won't have it." Peering at Belle, she asked, "What's wrong with your face? You look like you've had a stroke. Have you?"

"I might have," said Belle in her most penitent voice. She didn't know what a stroke did to anybody who had had one.

"Aunt George," said Nettie, "Belle hasn't had a stroke. Why do you ask such a fool question? She's only eleven years old. How could she have had a stroke?"

"Age hasn't got much to do with what happens to us," stated Aunt George. "In this family we have all sure found that out, haven't we?"

Nettie put her lips together and didn't answer. On the way to the cemetery she made a point of excluding Aunt George from her bridge club invitation.

Mrs. Pruitt said that she appreciated being asked, but she didn't feel up to any socializing. She asked Nettie to stop at a florist's shop to buy flowers for Darwin's grave. The car's air-conditioning was on, so the ride was comfortable.

At the cemetery Nettie parked the car just outside its open gates, but only Belle and her mother got out. Nettie blew her nose on a tissue. "Mama, I can't go in there. I just can't. I'll wait here in the car for you."

"If you don't mind, I think I won't go in either this time," wheezed Aunt George. "I couldn't find my hat and without it I get the headache, so if you don't mind, I'll wait here with Nettie."

Mrs. Pruitt said she didn't mind. She and Belle left the car, went through the gates and made their way to Darwin's grave site. It was a hot walk. They didn't talk. Between the long sad lines of the graves there were drifts of loose white sand. Belle carried the flowers, red roses in a florist's vase, their leafy stems embedded in a lump of clay.

Darwin's grave site was covered with a marble slab inscribed with the date of his birth and death. For a silent moment Belle stood beside it, stood close to her mother with her head reverently bowed. Then her mother took the vase of flowers from her and knelt to place it in the center of the slab.

"Red," said Belle. "He liked anything red. Remember his little red fire truck?"

Still kneeling, her mother looked up at her. She held her fist against her mouth, then dropped it. "If only I could believe this isn't the end. If only I could think he's somewhere. That's what I'm supposed to believe. That's what I've been told I must believe. So why can't I? Why can't somebody show me how? Or where?"

Tragically inept, Belle said, "I don't know, Mama."

Mrs. Pruitt rose and drew her neck scarf up around her twisted face. "Of course you don't. How could you? You're so young. I shouldn't have asked you. Please forget that I did and let's go now," she said. On the way back to the car she kept her eyes on the gate. Belle had to walk fast to keep up with her.

Nettie and Aunt George had been arguing. They didn't say so, but their faces did. So the return trip to the Pruitts' house was uncomfortable. Aunt George said why did Nettie have to have the radio on. Mrs. Pruitt was indifferent to the radio and to Belle's attempts at conversation. At the Pruitts' front door she got out of the car and thanked Nettie. To Belle she said, "Be good."

Aunt George heaved herself out of the car's backseat, but before she slammed its door, she poked her head back in and said to Nettie, "So you see how it is? Do you see now how it is, Missy?"

"Yes," retorted Nettie, "I see how it is. But I also see that you aren't making it any better. Mama is not sick, and I wish you'd stop treating her like she is."

"She's sick," said Aunt George, and slammed the car door.

Nettie didn't have her bridge club meeting the next day. Hamp came home that evening and in his clipped way announced that he was going to North Carolina the next morning on some factory business. He said he would probably be gone a week and didn't ask Nettie to go with him. He told her that she would.

So Nettie pasted a smile on her pretty face and went into a telephone huddle, first with Mr. Pruitt and then with Taylor. The upshot of this was that at nine o'clock Nettie drove Belle out to Holland's Dairy to stay with Taylor and Arlene in their cabin in the woods.

Chapter Four

IT STOOD to itself just off a sand road that ran around and past the dairy owner's big house, past barns, other outbuildings and spreads of fenced cattle range. All around the cabin there were tall pines that swayed and sighed and released their brown needles. The slightest air motion would set them to sighing, and the sound of this was wistful, like something yearning for something it didn't have.

The cabin had only one bedroom, so during her stay with Taylor and Arlene Belle slept on the couch in their front room. Its outside door opened out to a narrow porch, and beyond its single step there was bare ground, bare except for its covering of slick pine needles.

"If you could find out how to do it, you could make baskets out of all those pine needles and sell them," Belle told Taylor. "Everybody likes baskets. You could get rich. Then you wouldn't have to be an accountant."

Again at his correspondence studies, Taylor had brought his books to the kitchen table and was preparing to settle down to an evening of study, "I don't want to make baskets out of pine needles," he said. "I want to be an accountant." Arlene brought him another cup of strong coffee and, with a conspiring look for Belle that meant "You come too," tiptoed away.

The coffee didn't keep Taylor awake beyond his regular bedtime. After an hour of study he rubbed his red-rimmed eyes, closed his books and headed for bed.

Each morning Taylor rose at four o'clock,

[77]

ate a solitary breakfast and left for work. Arlene and Belle got up four or five hours later. They were in no hurry to do anything in particular. They ate cold cereal, and Arlene talked about When Taylor Finishes His Accounting Course.

When that happened, Taylor and Arlene were going to become owners of a home in the best part of Cold Springs. It was going to have a swimming pool and a garage that would hold two cars. Taylor was going to join one of those clubs that professional men belong to. He and Arlene were going to "be somebody" and act like they were. When Taylor came to the dinner table, not the supper table but the dinner table, he was going to wear his smoking jacket. Arlene was going to get it for him. It was going to be maroon velvet with black satin lapels.

"Taylor doesn't smoke," said Belle.

"Don't you think I know that?" said Arlene. "Even if he wanted to, he couldn't afford rabbit tobacco on what he makes now."

As the Deuce in what had been her parents' Two Aces and a Deuce chimpanzee act, Arlene had lived the greater part of her life traveling around the country with Little Beaver's Circus. Also traveling with Little Beaver's outfit had been a qualified teacher. From him Arlene had learned the things children in school classrooms learn. She had been educated further by clowns, snake charmers, rope artists, magicians and the movies. She had been the darling of the circus. Before Taylor she had never thought of wanting to be anything else. But then one quiet night when there was a watery moon, she put on her red dress, sneaked away from the circus camp, looked in on a place where there was dancing and met Taylor. She gave him her heart. He still had it, only now the happiness in handing it over to him was a little tired, a little dim.

Arlene's father used to come bare-chested to his supper table, but from the movies Arlene knew what gentlemen wore when they did. "A dinner jacket," she informed Belle, "is a dressy jacket gentlemen wear when they're at home. They don't have to smoke to own one."

"Then it shouldn't be called a smoking jacket," stated Belle.

Arlene carried her empty cereal bowl to the sink. Because the sink leaked, a bucket had to be kept under it. Because the cabin's windows wouldn't stay up when they were raised, they had to be propped with boards. The cabin had many annoyances. Nothing in it was right, so Arlene spent much of her time away from it. She didn't look for beauty in the woods. To her they were harsh. So when she walked in the woods, it was the soaring birds she looked for. They were so free.

Waiting for Arlene to dress for a walk in the woods, Belle sat on the cabin's porch watching the cows in a far pasture. The world was full of things that moved, or didn't move, and all of it was so simple and natural. To look at it and be satisfied that there was nothing more to it than what was seen was the only way to get along in it. It was best to forget its faults and not to look for answers to its questions.

Wind stirred the tops of the pines and more of their brown needles fell. The wind mourned their loss. The cows in the distance moved at a leisurely pace. They were cows so they didn't think about yesterday or tomorrow. Lucky cows.

Arlene came out onto the porch, and Belle brought her feet down from its railing and stood. A walk in the woods wasn't her idea of something to do but neither was sitting on a porch looking at cows.

Under a dazzling sky the woods lay tough, fertile and adventuresome. There were vine-clad bushes, patches of flower color where wild bees thrummed and trees that stood so close together they locked branches.

On a ground swell there was one tree that stood alone, and it caught Belle's attention.

[81]

It stood fifty feet tall, and under it there was a smaller one of its own kind. The branches of the taller tree hung brown and lifeless, its bole charred, its bark stripped cleanly away. Arlene said it had been struck by lightning, and watching for the birds, she walked on.

Alone under the taller tree, Belle looked up into its deadness and then looked down to see, thrusting up from its base, some green suckers. She leaned to touch the suckers and, as if prodded by some inner mystical voice, turned her head to gaze at its thriving fledgling. The air above both trees and all around them glittered.

Listening to the inner voice, Belle put a finger to her lips and stood motionless. She was still standing that way when Arlene came swinging back.

Arlene asked, "What's the matter?"

"It's this tree," said Belle.

"I thought a bee had stung you," said Arlene.

Belle dropped her hand. "I heard a voice."

Startled, Arlene looked around. "Whose voice? Where?"

"It was this tree," said Belle. "It spoke to me."

"I certainly hope you'll be careful who else you tell that to," said Arlene.

Belle ran all the way back to the cabin. The sun said it was noon.

Taylor came an hour later with what he said was news. "I had to go to town for Mrs. Holland this morning, and I stopped to see Mama and Aunt George."

"That isn't news," said Arlene.

Grinning, he said, "This is. We can take Belle home now. Ronald's father sent for him to come to West Virginia. Yesterday Aunt George put him on a bus."

"After all these years Ronald's father wants him?" exclaimed Arlene. "I never thought that would happen. I wonder how Aunt George made it happen."

"Probably she's been feeding Uncle What's-His-Name some pretty fancy stuff about

[83]

Ronald," exulted Taylor. "I'd bet a horse she got him to thinking he's getting a choirboy. Anyway, Ronald's gone."

"Goody," said Arlene. "Then go on and take Belle home, but don't stop for anything on the way. She isn't feeling well."

Taylor bent an examining look on Belle. "You're sick?"

"I am not sick," protested Belle. "I feel fine."

"She's hearing voices," said Arlene.

"What voices?" asked Taylor.

"It was only one," confessed Belle. "It belonged to a tree."

"What tree?"

Embarrassed of her belief, yet staunch of it, Belle looked into Taylor's disbelieving face. "A mother one. It's hurt. Lightning struck it but it isn't going to give up. It's growing again. It spoke to me."

Taylor didn't ask what the tree said. He told Belle to pack up her things and take them out to the pickup. On the way into Cold

Springs he said that she had better learn to stay out of the sun, that too much of it had queer effects on some people. In front of the Pruitts' house he said, "Tell Mama that Arlene and I will see her either Saturday or Sunday," and roared off.

Aunt George had come to the front door. Like a visitor waiting to be asked inside, Belle endured her heavy-lidded scrutiny. After a couple of seconds of this she said, "Taylor said I could come home, Aunt George. He said Ronald's gone to visit his father."

"Yes, Ronald's gone," said Aunt George, and stood back from the doorway.

Belle went past her, set her things down in the hall and went into the living room. Her mother was sitting in the chair in front of the silent television set. She had the family photograph album in her lap and was looking through it.

"Mama, I'm home," said Belle.

Her mother's smile was soft. It was a mother's welcoming smile but it didn't quite reach her eyes. What was in her eyes looked drained. She closed the album and put it aside. "Taylor said he was going to bring you. I'm glad you're home. It's been kind of strange here without you."

Belle sat down on the hassock beside her mother's chair. She was excited and in a hurry to tell what she had to tell, what she must tell, but *how* to tell it, how to make the personal side of it understood was the skittish question. In a fever to get to the telling of it, Belle reached for her mother's hand and held it in both of her own. "Mama, I went to the woods with Arlene this morning."

"Aunt George and I went to the cemetery," said Mrs. Pruitt. "The taxi we usually take to go out there couldn't come. We had to take what was sent, and we had to wait and wait for it to come back for us."

"And I saw a tree that lightning hit," said Belle.

"You're hurting my hand," said Mrs. Pruitt.

Belle dropped her mother's hand and sat

on both of her own. "I thought it spoke to me," she said. But then she fell silent because Aunt George had bustled in to say it was time for Mrs. Pruitt to make herself pretty for Mr. Pruitt, that today he would be home early.

"A husband that's been hard at work all day needs to come home to a wife that's all fresh and pretty," said Aunt George. "So you go make yourself that way. Go put on your blue dress and a little lipstick and brush your hair. Shoo! Skip now. I've got a cold supper planned, and after we eat it, you and I will go for our walk."

Mrs. Pruitt did whatever Aunt George told her to do. On her own she either could not or would not act. It was as though she had lost the ability to find the things of the world on her own, as though she intended to stay hidden from life as much as possible.

Aunt George made it possible. She met callers and peddlers at the front door and sent them away. She kept the house in rigid order and made all the household decisions. At mealtimes she sat in the chair at the head of the table dominating the table talk, directing the passing of the platters and bowls, and beaming her pleasure when someone thought to compliment her on her cooking. The kitchen was her domain. Mrs. Pruitt was allowed to sit in it, and talk and drink coffee, but was not allowed to wipe a dish or peel a potato.

For three days Belle furtively observed all of this. From the porch in the evening of the third day, after supper, she and her father watched Aunt George and Mrs. Pruitt start out on their walk. Aunt George, with her arm around Mrs. Pruitt, was guiding her and pointing at things for her to look at.

Wanting to run after them and yank her mother away from Aunt George, Belle sat sprawled on the top step of the porch. Over on the weedlot there was dusk life. Eyes peeped out of holes. Nocturnal creatures croaked and flapped. Skimming fireflies put on their lights. Up closer to the porch, a mockingbird in the loquat tree pulled out all the stops in its repertoire.

"Peace," remarked Mr. Pruitt. "It's what everybody is after but not everybody gets. We've got it though, haven't we?"

"Yes," said Belle, wallowing in peace. "We've got it." She wanted to get up and start a fight with peace, to whack it in its empty face, to make it go away and put something with some life in its place.

"That was a good idea you had about having Aunt George come to stay with us," said Mr. Pruitt. "She and your mother get along, don't they?"

Listening to the sound of a train hooting its distant way, Belle put her chin in her hand. "Yes, sir. They get along."

A pant of wind from some removed place, from just over that little hill down the road maybe, from where a bird had dropped a seed maybe, and where now there grew a new young life, brought a light sweet scent to the porch.

[89]

Breathing the wind, Belle sat up to look out across the lawn to the weedlot. "See?" beseeched the wind. "See?"

The night was coming, and Mrs. Pruitt and Aunt George were coming back from their walk. As if Mrs. Pruitt wouldn't know where next to put her feet unless she was told, Aunt George still had her arm around her, was still guiding her.

The mockingbird hadn't let up. Master mimicker of the songs of other birds, it twittered, whistled, chirped and trilled.

"That's comical," said Mr. Pruitt. "Isn't that comical." It wasn't a question, so he didn't expect an answer.

He didn't get one because Belle wasn't listening to him or to the bird. She was listening to her heart. It spoke, and with a flare in her eyes, Belle listened.

Chapter Five

THE VOICE of her heart slept with her
and woke with her. By the honest light of
day it was still with her, but by the honest
light of day there had to come some answers
to some down-to-earth questions.

Standing in the center of the Pruitts' ugly
weedlot that took up where their lawn left
off, Belle thought some long hard thoughts.
She pulled a weed and knocked the dirt from
its roots. On her bare head she could feel the
heat from the sun doing queer things to her
brain. A cagey thought came.

Belle put on a humble face, went back to

the house and was especially nice to Aunt George. "Has Ronald written you a letter yet?"

"Ronald doesn't write letters," said Aunt George. How could he, she asked herself, when he can barely write his own name?

"He should write you a letter so you'd know if he got to West Virginia," said Belle.

Aunt George took another of Mr. Pruitt's shirts from the basket on the table, shook it out, spread it on the ironing board and applied the tip of her iron to its collar. "He got there. His daddy sent me a telegram."

All sparkling innocence, Belle asked, "How long is he going to stay with his daddy?"

"I don't know," answered Aunt George, who had never let the sin of lying interfere with plans for herself. She had a plan now, and it did not include Ronald. It scared her a little because if it worked out the money orders from Ronald's father would stop, but by the time that happened, she would have money in the bank and would be a permanent member of the Pruitts' household.

Aunt George finished ironing Mr. Pruitt's white shirt, folded it, stood her iron on end and said, "Whew. It sure takes a lot of doing to keep this family looking decent."

"You want me to iron?" said Belle.

Aunt George fished Mr. Pruitt's tan shirt from the basket, shook it out and spread it on her board. "No, thanks. I want it done right."

"You want me to fix you a glass of ice water?"

"No, thanks. If I want a glass of ice water I'll fix it. You go play."

"Play what?"

"Anything."

Belle made herself a glass of ice water and sat at the table drinking it. "I feel like making something," she said, hoping that her confiding tone would soften Aunt George.

It didn't. Said Aunt George, "Do you think you can?"

"Something beautiful," said Belle.

"I've been knowing you since you were

three days old, and I've never seen you make anything, unless it was a fuss over something you thought somebody had done to you," said Aunt George. "To make something takes talent."

"I know it," conceded Belle, "and I know I haven't got any. That's why I need to ask you if you'll make a cake for when the Sunshine Girls come."

"What Sunshine Girls?"

"The Sunshine Girls," explained Belle. "They're girls. It's a club I belong to. We're the Sunshine Girls. We help other people and we help each other. That's why I want to have a meeting of them here—so I can show them what I need some help with."

"You don't have to have a cake for that," said Aunt George. "If you've just got to feed them when they come, give them some peanuts or raisins."

"Isabel Clark's mother served pink angel food cake the last time we had a meeting at her house," said Belle, thinking that if she couldn't butter up Aunt George any other way, the rival cake would do it.

Aunt George was not to be buttered. She said it was all right with her if The Sunshine Girls came for a meeting but it would have to be held in the yard, and if Belle wanted to serve cake she would have to make it.

"I don't know how to make a cake," protested Belle.

"Then it's time you learned," countered Aunt George, knowing full well that she wasn't about to let Belle do any messing around in her kitchen.

Belle made her expression thoughtful. "Mama would make it for me if I asked her. She likes to make cakes."

"You're not to ask your mama to do anything for you," snapped Aunt George. "She's still fighting with herself, trying to get over one of the worst things that can happen to any woman. It's not easy for her. She may look like herself on the outside, but inside it's all pain. Some women never get over what's happened to your mama. Don't you realize that?''

"I realize it," said Belle.

"I can't imagine a girl your age not knowing how to make something as simple as a cake," said Aunt George. "You're almost old enough to be married. Has that ever crossed your mind?''

"One time somebody else told me that," said Belle, remembering. On a Halloween night she had gone out with Isabel Clark to trick or treat, a gleeful adventure until it turned grim. At the last house, after being asked if she wasn't ashamed to beg and threaten, and after being told that she looked old enough to be married, she had had a door slammed in her shocked face. She knew she wasn't anywhere near old enough to be married. That wasn't going to happen until she was about thirty. Then if she met somebody who thought the way she did, and he asked her to marry him, she might do it.

"Eleven is too young to be married," Belle

told Aunt George. "Anybody like me, eleven years old, should try out all of our own ideas before we get married and get somebody else's shoved off onto us."

"I married when I was fourteen, and my husband didn't shove his ideas off onto me," said Aunt George. Because the only one he ever had that was worth anything was the one about buying the house, and I could have done that by myself if he hadn't saddled me with Ronald, she thought.

Belle switched the subject back to the cake. "Are you sure you won't make a cake for my meeting with The Sunshine Girls?"

"I am double sure," said Aunt George.

"Then," said Belle, "I guess I'll serve my friends raisins or peanuts when they come, but I don't have any money."

Sourly Aunt George said for Belle to make up her mind which it was going to be, that she would put raisins or peanuts on her list so that when Belle's father went grocery shopping he could get one or the other.

"Peanuts," decided Belle, but didn't specify what kind. Her father brought the kind that had thin red skins. Belle put them in custard cups, and served them to The Sunshine Girls when they came two mornings later.

There were six of them, and they came on their bicycles and sat on the sun-parched grass in the front yard. They munched peanuts and said they were delicious. It was early, and they covered their yawns with their work-roughened hands. They weren't very talkative. In a soft way they said how sorry they were about Darwin.

When all of the peanuts had been eaten, the Sunshine Girl named Joy turned to Belle. "When you phoned us to come, you said you had an emergency. Where is it?"

Belle rose and pointed. "It's that lot over there."

The Sunshine Girls rose and looked out across the lawn to the weedlot.

"I want to get it all cleaned up so I can

plant stuff on it," said Belle. "I'm going to make it beautiful. I won't need any help to plant it, but I can't clean it up by myself."

Pure and bright, The Sunshine Girls sagely nodded. They smiled.

Belle shared their smiles. "So when can we start cleaning it? Today? Tomorrow? Or when?"

"The weeds are so tall," commented the Sunshiner named Mabel. "I don't think they can be pulled. I think they'll have to be dug."

"And after that they'll have to be hauled out to the road," said Joy. "That's the only way the trash man will pick them up. They'll all have to be hauled out to the road and put in piles."

Eagerly Belle said, "Yes, but with all of us working at it, that won't take long."

Taller than Belle, Isabel Clark had to lean to look into her eyes. "Honey," she murmured, "we're sorry, we can't help you."

Jolted, Belle said, "You can't? But you've

got to. We're The Sunshine Girls, and it's our creed to help each other. It's one of our laws that we've got to help anybody who needs it."

"Honey," said Isabel, "you remember that time you were supposed to help us clean the Spanish moss out of Mrs. King's trees?"

"I think," said Belle, "that's when I had my tonsil operation. Wasn't that when I had my tonsil operation?"

"We thought that's why you didn't come to help us," said Isabel. "That's what you told us. So when we got through with Mrs. King's trees, we brought you some flowers. Your mother said she didn't know where you were but we found you. You were in a ditch you dug over there where the weeds are, and when you saw us coming with the flowers, you jumped out of it and started hollering about how you forgot what day it was."

Belle returned Isabel's steady gaze. "I did forget. I meant to come."

"And then," continued Isabel, "there was

that time we washed cars to earn money for the animal shelter."

"We must have washed a hundred cars that day," said Joy.

"And you didn't show up," said Mabel. "You promise but you never do."

"You never show up for any of our work," said Isabel in a pleasant, friendly way. "So you see how it is now?"

Regretfully, painfully, Belle saw how it was. She stood accused, truthfully accused, and presently she stood alone.

In the loquat tree there was bird movement and bird song. The mockingbird was back, tuning up.

"For corn's sake!" cried Belle. "Don't you ever shut up?"

The bird didn't say if it did or didn't.

Belle gathered up the custard cups and carried them back to the house. Earlier her mother and Aunt George had breakfasted with her and Mr. Pruitt. Now they were in the kitchen drinking second cups of coffee and looking at some fresh pictures in the family photograph album. On one of their trips to the cemetery they had taken pictures of Darwin's grave site, and these had been pasted in the album.

Mrs. Pruitt was telling Aunt George that she wanted a marble lamb for Darwin's grave.

"Yes," said Aunt George with an agreeable look, "if it was my little baby out there all by himself, I'd want that too. One of those cute little cuddly lambs made out of pink marble."

Mrs. Pruitt wondered how much the lamb would cost.

Aunt George said she had no idea.

Mrs. Pruitt said that Nettie and Hamp were back from North Carolina and that she would ask Nettie to take her to see a monument maker. She asked if Belle wanted to see the new pictures.

"I'll look at them later," growled Belle. She didn't want to see the pictures and didn't want to hear any more about the cute little cuddly lamb. It might be cute but it wouldn't be cuddly if it was going to be made out of marble. It would be cold, with no life to it.

Intending to wash them, Belle set the custard cups in the sink and reached for the box of dishwashing soap.

Aunt George glanced up, got to her feet and came to the sink. "Oh, no, my dear. Don't you bother with that. That's my job. You run on and play with your friends."

"They've gone," said Belle. I am not your dear, she thought. Nobody here is. You don't fool me. "My friends didn't want to play," she said.

"Then go play by yourself," said Aunt George. "I wish play was all I had to do. I'd be out there in a minute. Nobody would have to ask me twice. You want to change places with me?"

"I would but I've got more serious things on my mind," said Belle.

Aunt George turned and winked at Mrs. Pruitt. "She's got serious things on her mind."

Indulging her, as though Belle were six years old again, Mrs. Pruitt asked, "What serious things have you got on your mind?"

"You'll see," answered Belle, and stalked back outside to the shed where her father kept the yard tools. He wasn't particular about the condition in which he kept them because he wasn't a fancier of yard tools or lawns. Since the coming of Aunt George, he hadn't been bothered with the care of either because she had taken over the outside work, a job that she insisted was hers.

Aunt George didn't care for grass or for other growing things. When she mowed, she set the blade of the mower as low as she could get it, so the result was a scalp job. But that didn't discourage the grass. During the growing season it never quit.

This was the growing season, so now, on top of having to cut the Pruitts' idiot lawn, Aunt George had to go cut her own too. Hers was small but it was either go and cut it or allow her place to get a run-down look, and she couldn't have that. It had to be kept neat-looking so that if and when the time came for her to sell her house, there wouldn't be any bickering about the condition of the lawn. Keeping it neat meant that every five days or so she had to shuck out the money for a taxi to take her to her house and shuck out more for the return trip.

Thinking about the money she would get for her house if she decided to sell it and thinking about the money she wasn't going to have to shuck out on Ronald anymore, Aunt George ran hot water into the custard cups in the sink, added soap granules and started washing them. She began to tell Mrs. Pruitt about Ronald's father. "Last night I had a dream about him. I dreamed he asked me if he could keep Ronald for good. I told him I would have to think about it. I would too, if that ever really happened. I'd have to think about that a lot."

"Yes," said Mrs. Pruitt, "that would be a big step for you."

"It would just about kill me to give up my boy, but if it ever comes to that I think I'll have to do it. I'll have to think about him and forget about myself. I suppose I could get used to living by myself. Lots of women do."

"Have you ever thought of marrying again?" asked Mrs. Pruitt idly. "Lots of women do that too."

"No," said Aunt George, "I have never thought about that. In the first place, who would have me? I know I'm no prize."

"If you would fix yourself up a little and then get out and meet people, you might find someone who would think you were a prize," suggested Mrs. Pruitt. "You might find an older man looking for a woman like you, a good man needing somebody to make him a good home."

"You make that sound easy, but I know it wouldn't be," said Aunt George, rinsing the custard cups and setting them in the drain basket to dry. Her conversation with Mrs. Pruitt hadn't produced the offer she had hoped it would—an offer to move in with the Pruitts. She wanted one of them to be the first to suggest this. That it would happen she was confident, but there was no hurry, no hurry.

Finished with her job at the sink, Aunt George went to the door and looked out in time to see Belle, carrying a hoe and a spade, emerge from the tool shed.

On Belle's face there was a look of battle. There was nothing timid in the way she carried herself or her tools.

Chapter Six

MR. AND MRS. PRUITT told each other
that Belle's interest in making something of
the weedlot wouldn't last.

Belle herself was afraid it wouldn't. Each
morning when she opened her eyes to the
light, she expected it to be gone. There were
mornings when she wished for it to be gone,
and she would roll over and stare at the ceiling
and think about clearing a space on the far
end of the lot just wide enough and long
enough for another shirk ditch.

It made her laugh to think about the first
one, the delicious mischief of it. But then she

would sober and say to herself, "You know you're not ever going to have another one. You can't. It wouldn't be the same. Because then was then and now is now."

So, with a passionate sense of cause, Belle went each day to the weedlot and took up her spade and hoe. She set their blades into the earth, and when the roots resisted, when she couldn't free them with her tools, she dropped to her knees and tugged.

Under the roots ants toiled. There were swarms of gnats. The heat was sticky; the alarmed weeds shivered in its swelter. Their ground was being violated. They were doomed.

Belle stood beside a mound of uprooted wilting weeds and with a grimy hand scratched ant bites and swatted gnats. She had cleared about eight square yards of the lot, and for a beginning that would do. But what lay between the beginning and the ending should be for somebody with a stronger back than hers. Her back was miserable. Each time she lifted the hoe to chop and each time she knelt to pull was a fresh torture.

Belle left off swatting and scratching. She was going to be eaten alive or baked alive, and it didn't make much difference which. But she hoped that when her end came, there would be time enough for her to say a few words before she went. If there was, the words would be about Aunt George.

With a glint in her eye, Belle stooped and began hacking weeds from the ground, throwing them onto the pile with the others. She was hard at this when Nettie came.

Nettie wanted to know what Belle was doing.

"I'm cleaning this ugly place up so I can plant stuff where the weeds are now," said Belle.

"By yourself?" said Nettie. "You think you're going to clean this whole place up by yourself?"

"It's for Mama," said Belle.

Nettie said, "To get rid of all of the weeds

in here is an impossible job for one person."

Belle let fly with another weed. "Nothing's impossible."

Nettie fanned her face with her hand. "It must be close to a hundred degrees out here. People collapse in heat like this."

"I'm not going to collapse," declared Belle.

"Come go to town with Mama and me," said Nettie. "She wants to see about getting another marker for Darwin's grave, and then I'm going to take her to look at new wallpaper for Darwin's room"

"Mama doesn't want new wallpaper for Darwin's room," said Belle. "She wants it left like it is."

"I thought," said Nettie, "that she was getting over Darwin."

Belle moved to another stand of weeds and snatched up her hoe. She was panting. A gnat flew into her mouth and she spit it out. Ominously she said, "Listen. She's not getting over Darwin. She's not ever going to get over him as long as Aunt George is here. Aunt

George has got Mama in her clutches. Dad too. Not me, though. I've been watching her."

"You make her sound like somebody who needs watching," scoffed Nettie. "She doesn't. She means well. She gets on my nerves something terrible sometimes, but I've got to be fair about her. Underneath all of her crabbing and being so bossy, she means well."

"She doesn't mean well," said Belle, hacking away at weeds. "She means something else."

"What do you think she means?" inquired Nettie.

"I don't know exactly what yet," said Belle. "But I've been watching her and I've got this feeling. It's like when I know the answer to something before I look to see what it is, only I don't know how I know it. It's a feeling. Just like the feeling I've got about Aunt George. I'm not all the way onto her yet, but I will be pretty soon. The rest of you can think she means well if you want to, but I don't think it. I've got this feeling and I believe it. I believe myself. I know I'm right."

Nettie left her to her hacking, to the impossible.

Every yard gained was a fierce triumph over the impossible. Fiercely the weeds clung to the earth. The stronger ones had to be pried out, and all had to be put in grocer's boxes or bags and lugged out to the roadside for trash pickup.

Belle had a conversation with Aunt George about potato peelings, apple parings, orange rinds, wilted lettuce leaves, pieces of discarded cabbage and grass cuttings. "I want all of this stuff," she said, fishing long twists of apple parings from the kitchen garbage pail. "I want anything you throw away when you're cooking."

Aunt George muttered things to her paring knife.

"And when you mow the lawn, will you save the grass cuttings for me?" persisted Belle.

Aunt George raised her head to give Belle a slow look. "They have to be raked up."

"When you mow, I will go behind you and rake them up. I need them," said Belle, and scurried back to the weedlot. In a cleared, out-of-the-way place she began building a compost pile that day, and every day after that added something to it: more kitchen refuse, grass cuttings on mowing day, a spadeful of dirt, a pailful of water. When the pile was about six inches deep, she went to her father with the problem of commercial fertilizer and seeds.

She chose the wrong time and the wrong place for this. Her father and Aunt George were in the bathroom. He was seated on the edge of the bathtub and she was squatted before him trying to convince him that the way to cure an ingrown toenail was first to cut it back and then make a little hole in its center. She held his bare foot in her hand and was preparing to operate.

Mr. Pruitt was resigned, willing to do anything to get rid of the offending nail. He was not willing to listen to talk of money for fertilizer or seeds. In answer to Belle's request for it, his answer was an emphatic no. But the next day Aunt George came to the weedlot with an offer.

She stood with a plump hand on a broad hip and said, "I won't give you any money for your fertilizer or seeds, but if you want to earn it, I've got a fair proposition."

"What proposition?" asked Belle.

"You can go to my house and mow my yard every week," replied Aunt George. "I'll pay you three dollars each time you go."

Belle looked up from her digging to meet Aunt George's bland gaze. She knew that the proposition was not a fair one, that even the town wanderer, a harmless old derelict who sometimes came around begging for yard work, charged ten dollars for small lawns and twenty for big ones. Still, an unfair proposition was better than no proposition.

Her father saw nothing wrong with it. He

said that the trouble with the kids of Belle's generation was that they climbed out of their cradles with their mouths open and their hands stuck out expecting people of his generation to fill both. He said that he had found out what work was when he was nine years old, that it wouldn't hurt Belle to find out about it now, that it wouldn't kill her to get out and earn an honest dollar for some honest work.

To make his honest dollar for some honest work, Mr. Pruitt left home at six thirty A.M. every workday. Sometimes in the afternoons, on his way home, he drove miles out of his way to stop at Aunt George's place to pick up her mail left by another carrier and to make an outside check of her house, making sure it was still snug and safe. There was no time for that in the mornings, so on the days Belle earned her honest dollar she walked to Aunt George's place.

Aunt George's lawn mower was like the Pruitts', an elderly push-and-pull model without a catcher for grass cuttings. Belle decided against saving the cuttings for her compost pile. Those from her own yard would be enough for that. Those from Aunt George's yard she raked out as far as the edge of the road and left them there for the rain to wash away.

As she worked at this for the first time she was interrupted by rain. It was only a passing shower but it forced her to run for the cover of Aunt George's front stoop. She was standing there watching the rain disappear when the house looker came. He left his car parked in the road and walked across the sheared wet grass to the stoop.

He had the look that door-to-door salespersons have. To spare him the trouble of delivering a useless spiel and to spare herself the annoyance of listening to it, Belle quickly set him straight. "I can't buy anything. I don't live here."

The looker said that his name was Herbert Brown and that he was looking.

"Looking for what?" asked Belle.

"For a house to buy," answered Herbert Brown. "I've been all over Cold Springs looking at everything else that's available, but I keep coming back to this place. I know it isn't for sale now, but the lady who owns it told me that she was planning to sell it. I drove past here one day and caught her here working in her yard. I stopped and we talked a little, and that's what she told me."

To the air, Belle said, "I knew it. I knew it."

"What?" said Herbert Brown.

"I'm only the yard girl. I don't know anything about this house," said Belle.

"Well," said Herbert Brown with a last covetous look, "if it is put up for sale, I hope I get first crack at it."

Later on, had she been asked to do so, Belle could have described Herbert Brown in detail except for his name. She remembered that it was the name of a color but didn't remember that it was Brown until during supper that evening when Aunt George started talking about painting the Pruitts' house. "Wouldn't you like it to be a different color? Aren't you tired of looking at it white?"

Mrs. Pruitt looked up from her plate. "It's always been white."

"But not dirty white like it is now," reasoned Aunt George. "Picture it a nice warm brown with white trim. I could trim the windows in white. That'd look real pretty against the brown."

"Are you saying that you want to paint the whole outside of this house?" marveled Mr. Pruitt. "By yourself? But that's a man's job."

"I'm a better house painter than any man you ever saw," said Aunt George. "No man paints my house. I do it myself and you see how it looks."

"It's a doll's house," commented Mrs. Pruitt sincerely.

"I'm not lonesome for it," said Aunt George.

[119]

"What with Ronald gone I've lost my feeling for it. I don't think about it being my home anymore. It's just my house."

Mr. Pruitt said that he understood. "But when Ronald comes back, I'm sure you'll feel differently."

Aunt George looked brave and wan. "I've got a funny feeling about Ronald coming back. It's mysterious. It keeps telling me he isn't coming back. It keeps telling me his daddy is going to want to keep him and that I'm going to have to give him up. I tell you, if that happens it'll just about finish me off. I don't know how I'll keep going."

"You'll keep going," said Mrs. Pruitt. "You'll have to. All of us have to. No matter what happens to us, we all have to keep going. Somehow."

"I'm not thinking about the money I wouldn't get any more for Ronald's support," said Aunt George. "I might have to sell my house and go live in one room somewhere and eat dog food, but I could do that.

I'll get along. If I can't do it any other way, I'll take in washing. You all will let me do your washing and ironing, won't you? I work cheap."

"How cheap?" asked Mr. Pruitt, going along with Aunt George's banter.

"Cheap!" bellowed Aunt George, and everybody except Belle laughed. After supper she sat on the porch with her father and watched her mother and Aunt George start out on their evening walk.

Mr. Pruitt looked out into the green encroaching dusk. "I should go with your mother when she wants to take a walk, but she doesn't want me. She wants Aunt George."

"Because Aunt George talks to her about Darwin," criticized Belle. "She talks and talks to Mama about Darwin."

Mr. Pruitt came back with a sharp response. "Maybe it helps your mother to talk to somebody about Darwin. I'm no good at it."

"Aunt George is very good at it," said Belle.

[121]

"She's good at everything," said Mr. Pruitt. "She's a good woman."

"She likes it here with us," ventured Belle in an even tone. "I was wondering if she'd move in here with us if Ronald doesn't come back. I was wondering if she'd want to do that. Would you let her?"

Mr. Pruitt rested his head against the back of his chair. "Probably. But that's not going to happen. What Aunt George said while we were eating our supper was all kidding. She'd fight the Supreme Court before she'd let Ronald's father keep him. And as for her selling her house, that's not going to happen either. Next to Ronald, her home is her dearest possession. You ought to know that. It isn't as if you had just met her day before yesterday. Don't you know her?"

"I know her," said Belle, pulling her lower lip into her mouth and chewing on it. I know her better than the rest of you do, she thought, and that's peculiar, because I'm not as smart as the rest of you.

Chapter Seven

FROM THE WEEDLOT, watching as a
soldier at a listening post watches enemy
movement, Belle watched Aunt George paint
the Pruitts' house.

Every once in a while Mrs. Pruitt came
from the house to stand and look and offer
to help. Aunt George declined the offers, saying, "Honey, this is no job for a little thing
like you. You go on back in the house and
watch your programs."

"I'm a little tired of my programs," said
Mrs. Pruitt.

For all of her bulk, Aunt George was agile

and surefooted on her ladder. "Then work on those contests you said you were going to enter."

Mrs. Pruitt said she hadn't been able to think of a good slogan for any of her contest entries.

"Because you're not in the habit of contests yet," consoled Aunt George. "It takes a while to get the hang of it, but the first time you win one, you'll get the hang of it quick. One time I knew a woman who won two in one week. She got a fur coat and went to Las Vegas, Nevada, for three days. Before that she was like you are. She couldn't think of slogans either, but after she got the fur coat and went to Las Vegas, it was like she got another brain too. She could rip them answers to contests off in nothing flat. She won too. Regular."

Mrs. Pruitt said that she had never wanted to go to Las Vegas and that she preferred cloth coats to fur ones, that she thought to kill furry animals only to satisfy the vanities of women was criminal.

"If you win a trip to Las Vegas," said Aunt George, expertly wielding her brush, "give me the ticket and I'll go in your place. And if you win a fur coat, you don't have to wear it. You can sell it."

Mrs. Pruitt wandered away from the house. For a restless, helpless minute she stood under the loquat tree before walking over into the weedlot where Belle was working.

It was July, hot and still, and now the lot was mostly bare of weeds. The newly fertilized compost pile was decaying. When Mrs. Pruitt went past it, she said, "Phew."

Belle was spading, turning the black dirt to the light the way the man in the seed-and-fertilizer store had told her it should be turned. She saw her mother coming, and her eyes sought the box of seed packets sitting at the end of one furrow, but she continued to dig and turn, dig and turn.

From windows, whenever she remembered to, Mrs. Pruitt had watched what was going on in the weedlot. Only vaguely had it interested her. Only now, in a detached way, was she interested in it because it concerned one of her children. She disliked being out in the sun, and earth dirt had always been something she had been able to do without.

Mrs. Pruitt was wearing her sunglasses. Behind them her eyes took in the whole scene. She told Belle how changed the whole place looked.

"It's going to look more changed as soon as I get it all planted and everything starts growing," said Belle. Her spade hit a nest of pebbles. She threw the spade to one side, knelt and began cleaning the nest out with her bare hands.

Her mother moved down to the end of the furrow, stooped and lifted a packet from the seed box. She was uncurious about it and uninterested in it, but Belle thought that her mother, standing there holding the seed packet, was the most beautiful sight she had ever seen. She plunged her hands into the hole where the pebbles had been and with her fingers made three seed holes. "I'm going to plant this first row now. You want to help?"

"Oh, I don't think so," said Mrs. Pruitt.

"Fifteen minutes," coaxed Belle. "It won't take any longer than that to plant this whole row. Easy. Nothing to it. It goes quick." The expression on her face was intense, and excitement made her voice crack a little.

Mrs. Pruitt held out for another couple of minutes. Then she came, squatted beside Belle, opened the packet of seeds and tilted it against her palm.

Belle leaned, picked a seed from her mother's palm, dropped it into one of the finger holes and covered it over with dirt. Firmly and simply, she said, "When it grows it will talk to you."

Mrs. Pruitt moistened her dry lips with her tongue. "Yes," she said. "Of course." That evening when Mr. Pruitt came home from work, she told him she was worried about Belle. "She hasn't got a friend. Not one. That's what all that business over in the lot where the weeds were is all about. That's why she's seeding it. She thinks that when her seeds grow and become plants, they will talk to her. All those little girls she used to pal around with don't come here anymore for some reason. It breaks my heart."

Mr. Pruitt kissed his wife. "Don't let it. If Belle wanted friends, she'd have them. There's nothing backward about that kid."

"Seed," mourned Mrs. Pruitt. "That's all she thinks about. I gave her some money to spend on herself and she spent it all on seed. She's changed so during these last few months I hardly know her."

Mr. Pruitt put his hands on his wife's shoulders, brought her up out of her chair, steered her out to the front door and down the steps. They stood on the lawn looking at their house. Against its new coat of toast brown, its white trim glistened. The Pruitts were lavish in their praise of it.

Nettie came without Hamp, and Taylor came without Arlene. Nettie was so pleased with the looks of the house that she actually hugged Aunt George. "Now it looks like somebody of some account lives here," she said.

Taylor carried the ladder back to the tool shed. At the spigot in the front yard he took Belle's bucket from her and carried it over to the weedlot. Out of the corner of his eye he watched Nettie drive off.

He and she had never had much to say to each other except "How are you?" and "How is it going?" Every so often when they ran into each other, Nettie would ask Taylor when he was going to pay Hamp the money he owed him. Since he didn't know, Taylor would have to say so. Then Nettie would put a withering look on her face. At family gatherings she and Taylor were dutiful about being

[129]

friendly because neither wanted to be accused of being a spoilsport. But not once had Taylor and Arlene been invited to Nettie's home, and not once had Nettie and Hamp been invited to the cabin in the woods at Holland's Dairy. Taylor knew that Nettie could hardly stand him. He could hardly stand her.

Taylor could stand Belle. She didn't look down her nose at him. Now Taylor watched Belle, can in hand, dip water from her bucket. The earth was bare and thirsty. It had not yet begun to show any green.

Taylor had a criticism. "You're doing that the hard way. Why don't you use the hose? It'd stretch."

"The hose is all chewed up," said Belle. "Aunt George ran over it with the lawn mower, so now it leaks. I'm going to get a new one as soon as she pays me what she owes me for taking care of her yard. At first she paid me every week, but now I have to wait for my money because she has to wait for hers. Ronald's father sends her money every month, but now it's just dabs because Ronald is living with him and eats up the rest. She says she's going to do something about it and then she'll pay me."

Taylor made his lips thin, went to the tool shed, found a roll of heavy mending tape, returned to the front yard and spent thirty minutes trying to repair the mangled hose. It had to be spliced, and in the end there were still leaks, so the pressure of the water coursing through its skinny length was reduced. Belle pulled it over into the center of the lot and directed the thin stream from it into a wide deep hole.

As if he had never seen one, Taylor asked, "What is it?"

"It's a hole," answered Belle.

"If somebody came out here at night and didn't know it was here, he'd break a leg or his neck if he fell in it," said Taylor.

Belle explained. "The man at the seed and

fertilizer store said it had to be this big so when we put the tree in it its roots will have enough room to spread out."

"I have never given trees and their roots any consideration," said Taylor.

"And when we dig it up, we've got to take up plenty of dirt with it. We've got to wrap something around its roots so they won't be so shocked when we bring it from the woods."

"Woods? What woods?"

"Your woods."

"Those woods belong to Mrs. Holland," sputtered Taylor. "We can't go out there and dig up a tree."

"I know we shouldn't even try to dig up the mother one. It's hurt and we'd hurt it more if we tried to move it. But we can get the baby one. You can ask Mrs. Holland if she'd let us have it. She'll give it to us. I know she will. It's for Mama," confided Belle delicately. "When my seeds get to be plants they'll make her see what I want her to see, but the little tree will make her see it quicker."

Taylor eyed her. "I don't know what you're talking about, but a tree isn't going to make Mama see anything quicker. She doesn't need it."

For a long, silent and merciless moment Belle stared at him. Then her scream came. "Don't do it then! Don't help me! Don't anybody help me! Say I'm a lunatic and feel sorry for me! Tear up the hose and don't pay me so I can't buy a new one! Watch me but don't help! Paint the house! It's more important than what I'm doing! Think that if you want to! Run away if you want to! I don't care! I don't need you! I don't need any of you! I can get it all done by myself!"

"Aw, rats," said Taylor. To shut Belle up about the tree, he thought of offering her a dollar but he didn't have a spare one. There was only enough money in his pocket for the haircut he had promised Mrs. Holland he would get. She had ordered him to get it and had given him the afternoon off to do it. While he was in Dave's Barber Shop, Belle waited for him in the pickup parked across the street.

The haircut made him feel better. He looked better for it. On the way out to Holland's Dairy Belle told him so. "Now you don't look like a cow herder."

The pickup took a bump in the road. The spade and the shovel in its back end rattled.

"I don't look like a cow herder because I'm not one except temporarily," said Taylor stiffly. "Who said I was one?"

"It was Nettie," admitted Belle with a rueful twist of conscience. "But she didn't say it mean."

"She said it mean," declared Taylor. "Don't tell me she didn't because I know she did,"

Belle kept her eyes fixed on the road ahead. She didn't want to be drawn into any more tattling. She tried to think of something to say that would smooth things over but nothing came.

It was after five o'clock but the sun was still a long way from setting when Taylor pulled the pickup into Mrs. Holland's driveway. He went in to see her and was gone for fifteen minutes. When he came back out, he climbed into the pickup and slammed its door. "All right. I've got her permission to dig up the baby tree. We'll stop at my house for a piece of burlap to wrap its roots in, and then we'll go after it. But I want to tell you that after the tree, if you've got anything else in your mind for me to help you with, don't ask. Just don't ask. I'm a working man and I've got responsibilities. I don't have time to chase around after you and your play stuff."

Chapter Eight

THE TRANSPLANTED TREE had a hard time of it. Belle and Taylor had mixed compost with its holding soil. To get rid of air pockets, they packed soil around its roots. Belle built a dike around it so that its daily dousings wouldn't run off.

Reluctantly, her mother came from the house several times to look at it, and to muster a comment or two about it and about the spindly little seed growths that were just beginning to push up from the ground.

The growths were pale, and the fledgling tree looked sick. Some of its higher twigs turned brittle and yellow. Their leaves curled and fell. But one day in mid-August Belle broke off one of its lower twigs and saw beneath its bark a layer of fresh moist greenness.

She laughed aloud and sprinted back across the lawn to the Pruitts' front porch. Her father, her mother and Aunt George were there. Reading from his evening paper, her father was saying that squall lines were reported to be moving throughout the Gulf states.

"Squalls don't scare me none," said Aunt George. "The paper plays them up big but they lie. A little rain and some wind, that's all their squalls ever amount to."

On that day and at that hour the sky was clear except for the red sun and a few thin clouds. The wind was coming from its usual direction.

Mr. Pruitt looked at the sky and then at Belle. "We missed you at supper. Where were you? Over there wallowing in the dirt again? That's what it looks like."

With an air of folksiness, Aunt George said, "Our little girl loves dirt. She lives in it. It's her home. It's where she lives now. Isn't that right, Belle?"

Shifting her weight from one foot to the other, Belle stood beside her mother's chair. As if to explain some wise and secret quality in her character, she said, "I have to love dirt."

"Well, I guess that's harmless enough," said Mr. Pruitt. He transferred his attention from Belle to Mrs. Pruitt and Aunt George. "What did you two do today?"

"Nettie was supposed to have brought me some peaches," said Aunt George. "She said she'd bring me a bushel so I could start my canning tomorrow, but she didn't show up, so we went to the cemetery."

"The man from the monument place met us there with the lamb for Darwin's grave," said Mrs. Pruitt. "It's nice. I know you'll like it when you see it."

Leaning, Belle put her hand out to touch

her mother's cheek. "Mama, my tree isn't dead. It's growing."

"Your fingers are sticky," said her mother, "and you smell. Go take a bath and then go to the kitchen and eat your supper. I fixed a plate for you. It's on the back of the stove."

"It's a real nice marker," said Aunt George. She didn't say what she thought—that to spend money on anything as useless as a grave marker was idiotic. In her view things that cost money didn't belong in cemeteries. Money belonged in banks, which was where hers was going to go if or when she sold her house. Her July and August money orders from Ronald's father were going to go there too.

Both were made out for the usual, full monthly amounts and tucked away in her bottom dresser drawer. Aunt George treated herself to another look at the money orders before she climbed into her bed that night.

During the night, the sky over Cold Springs remained clear. The air was warm and muggy. The clouds were high and inactive.

Belle's mother didn't come to the kitchen for breakfast the next morning. Her father said that she was sleeping and was not to be disturbed. It was a Saturday and a workday for him. He left the house at six thirty.

During the morning, waiting for her mother to come from her room, Belle made many trips from the weedlot to the house. Under the relentless eye of Aunt George she drank many glasses of water, and tiptoed again and again to the closed door of her mother's room.

The last time she did that, Aunt George took her by her arm, pushed her to the back door and put her out. "And don't let me see your face in here again until lunchtime!"

"How will I know when that is?" asked Belle.

"I'll call you," said Aunt George, and tried to slam the screen door. It wouldn't slam because she had replaced its old spring with a new one.

Belle went back to work in the weedlot. Nearly all of it was beginning to show some life, but at the far reaches of it, in places that were beyond the stretch of the hose, life was frail. The new growths had sun but never enough water. Buckets and buckets of water had to be carried to them.

Noon that day came and went, and Aunt George did not call Belle to come to the house for lunch.

At one o'clock one of the most terrifying and dramatic of weather disturbances occurred. There was a sudden and rapid change of wind direction. The clouds grew black and lowered. Chased by violent winds, they began to boil. Within fifteen minutes the air temperature dropped fifteen degrees. There were great thunder explosions. Green lightning lighted the sky, flash after flash of it. In one hour two inches of rain fell. There was hail the size of Ping-Pong balls.

With her mother and Aunt George, Belle watched the squall from the Pruitts' living room windows. The strength of it lasted for an hour. The rain and hail were the first to go. Then the thunder and lightning stopped, and the wind blew an exhausted breath and went away.

Only then was it safe for Belle to leave the house and go to her plant lot. She stood in its center and with bitter eyes gazed at its ruin. The rain and hail had beaten her plants into the ground. Her tree had not survived its beating either. Uprooted, it lay on the ground. Her compost pile was gone.

The hurt of it all was too cruel and senseless for tears, so Belle did not weep.

That evening at supper she sat with her eyes downcast. Taylor and Arlene came by on their way to the movies. They said they could stay long enough for pie and coffee. Aunt George made places for them at the table.

Nettie had come with the peaches. She invited herself for supper. "There isn't going to be any at my house because Hamp is out of town. But even if he wasn't, I couldn't cook because the storm knocked out the electric service at my house. It's been out since a little after one o'clock. I suppose everything in my freezer is going to be ruined."

"Out our way we only got a little rain," said Taylor.

"We were lucky," said Mrs. Pruitt. "The storm didn't touch our electric service."

"Squalls are peculiar," said Mr. Pruitt. "They've been known to settle down in one place and beat it to a pulp, and only five miles away the sun will be shining."

Belle looked up from the food on her plate and in a dazed tone said, "The storm tore up my plants and my tree. They're all ruined. My compost pile is gone too. The wind blew it away."

Her stiff announcement was loud enough to be heard by everyone. They heard, and fell silent for a moment, blinking an instant's sympathy the way people do when they hear something they should be but can't be concerned about.

Her mother alone was genuinely concerned. "Oh, honey, I'm sorry. But why didn't you say something about this to me before now? Why didn't you tell me?"

"I don't know," said Belle. "You were working on your contests and I didn't want to bother you."

Her mother showed a little spirit. "It wouldn't have been a bother. But about the plants. You can plant more. Can't you plant more?"

"No," said Belle. "I'm done with seeds and plants. I can't go through all that again."

Mr. Pruitt thought that the best way to handle this situation was to be brusque. The stricken look on Belle's face moved him to generosity. "Oh, you can too. I tell you what. You clean up your plate, and then you and I will go and get you all the seed you want. We'll get you a hose too, a nice long one. I'll pay for everything. How would that be?"

Belle ducked her head. "No. It's too much. Seeds and plants don't mean anything. That's all they are. Seeds and plants. I'm through with them."

"Well, I for one don't blame you," declared Aunt George. She rose, went to the kitchen, came back with the coffeepot, waddled around to Mr. Pruitt's chair and leaned over his shoulder to refill his cup. "It was real sweet of you to stop at my house on your way home. I'd have been worried if you hadn't. I would have had to ask you or Nettie to run me over there for a look myself."

"Your house is fine," said Mr. Pruitt.

Still alone in her concern, Mrs. Pruitt said, "Eat your supper, Belle."

"Who wants pie?" asked Aunt George.

"Just a little piece for me," said Nettie. She wasn't through with her complaints about her freezer and the electricity. "I just stocked my freezer, and if everything in it spoils before the electricity comes back on, Hamp will go to city hall when he gets back and fill somebody's ear so full it will come out like a balloon on the other side. I don't know why we can't have better public services in this town."

Arlene took a dainty bite of her pie. "We don't have a freezer, so even if our electricity was off, we wouldn't have to worry about anything in it spoiling."

Nettie made a pitying point. "A freezer only costs two or three hundred dollars."

"We don't have two or three hundred dollars," admitted Arlene.

"You could have if you and Taylor didn't have to go to the movies every Saturday night," argued Nettie heatedly. "Hamp and I almost never go. Why do you and Taylor have to?"

Remembering the hundred and twenty-five dollars Taylor owed Hamp, Arlene looked guilty. "The movies are the only recreation Taylor and I have."

Nettie noticed the dress Arlene was wearing. "That's a pretty dress you have on. Did I give it to you?"

"A couple of years ago you did," said Arlene.

For the first time in his life and hers, Taylor

decided to put Nettie in her place. He had had enough of her and her pity. He had had just about enough of everybody, including himself. Earlier in the week he had gone to Mrs. Holland to ask for a raise and had been told he wasn't worth one. While in her office he had observed the little gray-cheeked, squint-eyed accountant who sat buried in mounds of paper at a makeshift work space at Mrs. Holland's desk. Peevishly going over her accounts, frantically feeding figures into his adding machine, frantically searching for errors and making corrections, he clucked and muttered to himself.

Taylor had spoken six words to him. "It's a nice day, isn't it?"

"I wouldn't know about that," snapped the accountant without a wasted glance. "I haven't had time to look." He looked like he had never seen the sun or drawn a breath of fresh air. Mrs. Holland didn't bother to introduce him to Taylor. To her, the accountant was no more than a utility.

Taylor's interview with Mrs. Holland had lasted only about three minutes. They were mind-awakening minutes. While they lasted, Taylor hadn't been able to keep his eyes from straying to the man at the desk, and the possible truth that one day he too would be nothing more than a utility to an employer hit him.

He had been immensely relieved to leave Mrs. Holland's office and go back to the sunny pastures and the cows. Since then he had begun to feel differently about his studies. When he could find the time and energy for them, they were going well enough, but now the very thought of going to them, of sitting for hour after hour in almost complete isolation, learning rules laid down by others, filled him with a sense of dread. He couldn't shake the memory of Mrs. Holland's account man. He knew that sooner or later he was going to have to tell Arlene that he had changed his mind about wanting to be an accountant, but he kept putting it off, waiting for just that right close moment to come. He had hoped that would be tonight, on the way home from the movies, but now that wasn't going to happen. Nettie was taking care of that.

Taylor was tempted to pick up what was left of his pie and paste Nettie in the face with it. Instead he turned to her and in an ugly voice said, "If you didn't hear what Arlene just said about the dress she's wearing, I'll tell you again. Yes, you gave it to her. Do you want it back?"

"I didn't say I wanted it back," said Nettie. "I merely asked her if it was one I gave her."

"I want you to have it back," said Taylor.

"I don't want it," said Nettie. "Why would I want it? I've got a whole closet full of dresses I've barely worn."

Taylor rose and stomped around the table to Arlene. "I want Nettie to have her dress back. Give it to her."

"Now?" faltered Arlene.

"Yes, now!" thundered Taylor. "Stand up and peel it off and give it to her!"

"Children!" said Mr. Pruitt. "Stop this."

"Yes," said Mrs. Pruitt. "Do stop."

"They hate each other," said Belle.

Mrs. Pruitt leaned to Belle. "Eat your supper, pet."

"I'm not hungry," said Belle in a quavering voice. "I want to be excused. May I be excused?"

"You should eat," said Mrs. Pruitt.

"Oh, for heaven's sakes excuse the child," said Aunt George. "If she doesn't want to eat she doesn't want to eat, but there'll be no raiding my refrigerator later on."

Taylor had jerked Arlene to her feet. "Take off the dress and give it to Nettie!"

"I won't!" shrieked Arlene. "We're going to the movies. I can't go in my underwear."

"We are not going to the movies!" shouted Taylor. "You're going to take off that dress and give it to Nettie, and then we're going home!"

"Take your hands off me!" cried Arlene. "You're hurting me!"

Aunt George made a placid suggestion. "Arlene, you can borrow one of my dresses to wear to the movies. Just don't forget where you got it. I want it back."

"One of your dresses would swallow me," moaned Arlene. "I'd look ridiculous in it and you know it."

"Then don't borrow it," said Aunt George.

"Arlene doesn't need to borrow your dress," drawled Nettie. "Taylor's just showing off. He's just being dramatic, showing off to the rest of us what a big man he is."

With such suddenness that she almost fell, Taylor released his hold on Arlene. Under its summer tan his face was white. He started back around the table to Nettie but didn't make it past Mr. Pruitt's chair. Pleading for peace, Mr. Pruitt put his hand out and stopped him. "Son, pull yourself together. You and Arlene both pull yourselves together. If you've finished here, go on and go to the movies."

"Yes," said Nettie, "why don't you do that? But before you haul out of here, get those peaches out of the trunk of my car and bring them in. I left the keys in the ignition. There's some other stuff in the trunk but it's mine. Just bring the peaches in."

"And the sugar," said Aunt George.

Nettie frowned. "Aunt George, I forgot the sugar."

Aunt George pounced. "You forgot my sugar? But how could you? I told you I needed it. I told you I was going to start my canning tomorrow."

"I forgot it," said Nettie, glaring. "You're lucky I remembered the peaches. I'm not your errand boy. Today has been terrible for me, just terrible, and it isn't over yet. I told you about my electricity being off. If it isn't on by the time I get home tonight I don't know about all the food in my freezer. It'll spoil, that's what, and I don't see anybody here helping me worry about it."

"Nettie," soothed Mr. Pruitt, "it takes a long time for a big freezer like yours to unfreeze. I doubt the food in it is going to spoil before your electricity comes back on."

"I don't see how you could have forgot my sugar," wheezed Aunt George.

"I'll go after your sugar," said Mr. Pruitt. He still had his hand on Taylor's arm, detaining him, but now he dropped it and rose. "Come on, Son. Let's get those peaches out of Nettie's car, and then you and Arlene go on and go to the movies if that's what you want to do."

The color had come back into Taylor's face. Fair-browed and churlish, in the way of a little boy, he hung his head. "I don't want to go to the movies. I want to go home."

"Then go," advised Nettie in a nasty tone. "Nobody's stopping you. Assert yourself if you can."

Arlene sent Nettie a furious look. "Taylor knows how to assert himself."

"I have never seen him do it," said Nettie.

Mrs. Pruitt began to rearrange everything

within her reach. In a voice that shook, she said, "There's a child in this house," but didn't complete what she had started to say because nobody was paying attention to her.

Mr. Pruitt was trying to make himself heard. "Children, children, what in the world has got into you, talking so hateful to one another? Come on now, be nice. Let's all be nice."

"I am nice," said Nettie.

"Ha!" screamed Taylor.

"Disgraceful," said Aunt George. "I'll remind you that you're at my table."

Mrs. Pruitt picked up her knife, her fork and her spoon and, holding them high, stood, opened her hand and let all three fall back down onto the table. The noise of this drew attention.

"Mama," exclaimed Nettie, "what are you doing?"

Like a mother bear that has been roused from a long tranquilizing cave nap, Mrs. Pruitt looked squarely into the faces around her table, *her* table, and in a voice that was terrible in its calm and authority, said, "Shut up. All of you shut up. I am not going to hear any more about dresses or peaches or sugar or movies. There's a child in this house and she's hurting. And what we are going to do about it is what we are going to talk about now."

Belle voiced a weak denial. "If I am the child you're talking about, I am not hurting."

"You'd better straighten your face and sit up there and eat your supper," said Aunt George. "It'll be tough berries if you don't and you get hungry later on. When I close my kitchen for the night, it's closed."

For that, Aunt George suffered Mrs. Pruitt's scathing look that spoke a volume.

The look that Mrs. Pruitt bent on Belle was clear. It too spoke a volume. "You don't have to eat now if you don't want to, pet. Maybe you'll be hungry when you and your father get back from the seed store. You'll feel better then. We'll have a little cozy snack in the kitchen, just your dad and you and I. Do you want me to go with you and your dad to the seed store? Come on, I'll go with you."

Aunt George said nothing more to Mr. Pruitt about going after the sugar for the peaches. A few minutes later, alone in the kitchen, she washed the dishes, and sulked until she remembered that she was a resourceful, intelligent woman.

Aunt George began to lay some new plans for herself. When the last dish had been dried and put away, she hung her dish towel on its rack, selected a peach from the basket near the door and went out onto the back porch to eat it. It was ripe and the juice from it ran down her chin.

Chapter Nine

S UNDAY CAME, and the members of the Pruitt family, all but Aunt George, met in Belle's plant lot. With considerable satisfaction Mrs. Pruitt noted that her adult children were much subdued.

Compliments of Mrs. Holland, Taylor and Arlene had brought another young tree from the woods at Holland's Dairy. They would have set about planting it in the hole where the first little tree had been, but Belle said, "No. I want to do it. Mama will help me."

Nettie said that the electricity in her house was on and that nothing in her freezer had spoiled. "Where," she asked, "is Aunt George?"

Mrs. Pruitt waved an airy hand. "Gone."

"Gone where?"

"Home. She was all packed up and ready to go when your father and I got up, so we took her."

"Ronald must be coming back," speculated Nettie.

"She didn't say if he was or wasn't," said Mrs. Pruitt. "She's going to get married again."

"Who is she going to marry?" asked Nettie.

"She doesn't know yet. She's going to fix herself up and then go out and find somebody," said Mrs. Pruitt. She was wearing one of Mr. Pruitt's old shirts and a pair of pants that had belonged to Taylor before he became a school dropout. The tails of the shirt hung almost to her knees, and on her the pants were shapeless, but Nettie had not a word to say about either. She, Taylor and Arlene took the tools Mrs. Pruitt handed up to them, went to the far end of the lot and started the job of smoothing the squall-ravaged soil. Mr. Pruitt chose his own tools and went out to work in the area nearest the road.

The eight o'clock wind was sweet and solemn. Here and there in the roughened earth were bits of drowned roots and stems that spoke of what had been and what could be, but Nettie did not hear the wind or see what the earth promised. Trying to estimate how long it would be before she could turn in her rake and go home, she turned every now and then to look at Taylor and Arlene. As they worked, they talked.

This was the time for which Taylor had been waiting. He began to tell Arlene what he had discovered about himself: that he would not become an accountant, that he couldn't sit chained behind a desk for the rest of his working life, that he had to work at something that would keep him out in the open, that he knew this might change the way Arlene felt about him. Almost in tears, he finished what he had to say. "I mean, I may never be able to give you the things you want. Maybe I'll never be anything more than a cow herder, so if you want to leave me, I won't blame you."

Arlene blinked and blinked again. For all of her eventless life in the cabin in the woods, her second-hand clothes and Taylor's paycheck that was never enough, she couldn't imagine her life without him. "Leave you?" she said. "But where would I go? What would I do?"

"You could find somebody else," answered Taylor.

"Yes," said Arlene after a slow moment, "I suppose I could." For her it was a noble moment. It was the kind that women the world over and for centuries have experienced when, in times of trouble, they find within themselves the strength to stand by their troubled men.

Arlene was a woman in love with her husband. For her, no matter what, there could be no other. So she said, "But I don't want anybody else."

Taylor wiped his wet eyes on his sleeve and told Arlene that he was going to ask Mrs. Holland for more job responsibility so that the next time he asked for a raise he'd get it. "And I'm going to fix up our cabin too. I'm going to fix everything that's wrong with it. The sink in the kitchen first. I don't know why I've let that sink go so long."

"Because," said Arlene with wifely patience, "you never had time before. Now you will."

For Taylor the world settled. He squared his shoulders and took a better grip on the handle of his rake.

Belle's world and her mother's was not yet settled. The squall winds had blown dirt into the tree hole, and then the squall rains had soaked it. Now Belle was emptying it to make room for the replacement tree. The dirt from her inexpert shovel flew up and out.

Her mother came to observe, and after a brief time of observing had a dry comment. "The way you handle that shovel doesn't thrill me."

"This dirt is wet," puffed Belle, "and it's heavy."

"Then maybe you should let it go until tomorrow," said her mother. "There is going to be one, you know."

"The tree doesn't want to wait till tomorrow. It wants to be planted today," said Belle.

Her mother turned to glance around at the common features of the outdoor day. And turned back to pull the tails of her shirt together and tie them. A small resolute figure, she hitched up her pants. "Well, all right, but I'm not going to stand here and watch you knock one of your eyes out. Give me that shovel."

So the hole was emptied, and after that Belle and her mother lifted the little tree from its burlap wrapping, set it in its hole and began to pack dirt around its roots.

Watching her mother's hands, wrist deep in the warm gritty soil, Belle made a statement. It was, simply and passionately, something that she had to say. For her it was truth. "Mama," she said, "Darwin is here."

Her mother's hands rested. On her knees, she sat back to regard the leafy branches of the baby tree and then turned her head to give Belle a long deep look.

"It is," said Belle. "This is where he is, Mama."

In a tremulous voice, her mother said, "Oh, Belle." Her lips formed more words but she didn't speak them.

The light from the climbing sun, the August sun, was strong and clean.

On the eighth of December Belle turned twelve. As his gift to her, her father took her to the Fashion Bootery for a pair of new shoes. She chose black ones with silver Pilgrim buckles.

Her mother had two gifts for her—a cooked-to-order birthday dinner and a secret to be shared with the family guests but not before the cake was served.

The calendar said that it was autumn, but autumn was fickle that year. There should have been a sense of finality to it, but to feel that and see it required a close eye. Day after yellow day the winds blew from the south, and the rains were warm and kind. The autumn was more like a spring. Every few days or so Belle's father wheeled the lawn mower out and cut the grass that wouldn't stop growing. Belle went behind him, raking up the cuttings to add to her new compost pile. The little tree in her weedlot stood clothed in shiny tender green. To make a centerpiece for the birthday table, she gathered lavender verbena from one of her flower beds.

Nettie, Arlene and Taylor came with presents: a ballpoint pen from Arlene and Taylor, and a cashmere sweater from Nettie.

Nettie had come primed for a feast of roast leg of lamb or escalloped oysters, but when she saw what she was going to get, she drew back in her chair. "Oh, now, what's this?"

"It's Belle's birthday dinner," said Mrs. Pruitt. "I told her we'd have whatever she ordered, and this is what she ordered."

"I don't think I'm hungry," said Nettie. "I'll wait for the cake."

"Belle has plebeian tastes," commented Mrs. Pruitt, unperturbed.

"I like plebeian food," said Taylor.

"Me too," said Arlene.

Happily Belle attacked her plate of liver and onions. Unhappily Nettie watched her for as long as she could bear to, and then began a conversation with Mr. and Mrs. Pruitt. "This morning when I was in the post office, I saw Aunt George. She was mailing Ronald's things to him. He's not coming back to live with her. That man she's married to now was with her. What's his name?"

"That's Uncle Shep," said Mr. Pruitt.

"Uncle Shep has got a face on him that would stop a clock," said Nettie. "No won-

[165]

der Aunt George is keeping him under cover. If I were married to somebody as sour-looking as he is, that's what I'd do. I'd hide him."

"I don't think Aunt George is hiding Uncle Shep," said Mrs. Pruitt. "They were married in a civil ceremony and now they're honeymooning, that's all."

"Aunt George told me that Uncle Shep is a retired railroader and that they are living in her house," said Nettie. "Wouldn't you just know she'd pick somebody named Shep? That's a dog's name. Isn't that a dog's name?"

"Nettie," rebuked Mrs. Pruitt. "Stop. This is Belle's birthday and this is her dinner."

"Then let's have the cake," said Nettie. "Can't we have the cake now?"

It was pink angel food, and when the twelve candles on it had been lighted, Belle blew them all out with one mighty breath. She tucked her chin, but then lifted it to look into the faces of her guests. "I made a wish."

With her fork Nettie carried a bite of her cake to her mouth. "Well, good luck. Personally, I never waste my time on wishes."

"Mama," said Taylor, "this cake is delicious."

"It certainly is," agreed Arlene. "Everything is just beautiful, Mother Pruitt. *You* are beautiful tonight. I've never seen you looking so well."

"That's because I feel well," murmured Mrs. Pruitt modestly. "I haven't felt as well as I do now in years."

"I want," said Belle to the room at large, "to tell what I wished for."

Nettie took another bite of her cake. "Then tell it. We're listening."

"Twins," breathed Belle. "A boy and a girl this time. Twins."

Nettie frowned. "A boy and a girl this time? What time? And what twins?"

"Twins!" cried Belle. "Mama is going to have a baby. That's what my wish was about. I wished for a boy and a girl this time. Twins!"

As if she had been punched in the stomach, Nettie said, "Uhhhh," and a little shriek like that of some strange animal came out of her mouth. She dropped her fork and had to get down under the table to search for it.

Taylor helped her find it. He picked it up and would have handed it to her, but Arlene said, "No. I'll get her a clean one," and skipped to the kitchen to stand in its comfortable gloom for a couple of seconds with both hands pressed to her cheeks. There weren't any clean forks. She had to wash and dry one. Nettie thanked her for doing that.

"You're so welcome," said Arlene, and, all glad-eyed and in a tone of wonderment, said, "Nettie. Nettie, there's going to be a new baby in our family. Isn't that wonderful? It's a miracle. Don't you think it's a miracle?"

The stunned look in Nettie's face disappeared. She grabbed Arlene's hand, raised it to her lips and in a misty voice said, "Oh, Arlene, it is. That's what it is. It's a miracle."

Mr. Pruitt got up, went around to Mrs. Pruitt's chair and kissed the top of her head.

She looked up at him and said, "You haven't eaten your cake. Go back and eat it."

Nettie took a piece of the cake home with her. Arlene and Taylor took two pieces. After they had gone, Belle and her mother and father went out to sit on their porch. Her mother talked about new wallpaper for the room that had been Darwin's.

The light on the porch was growing dim with the coming night. When it had fully come, the old house put its arms around those inside it and held them close.

Property of
Saint Mary School
Bethel, CT

F
CLE

CLEAVER, VERA
BELLE PRUITT